FORGET-ME-NOT

As girls, Diana Aspley and Alice Simmonds swore that they would be friends forever. So Diana is devastated when she receives the news that Alice has died in unexplained circumstances. Then during her first London Season, she thinks she catches sight of a familiar figure from a carriage window . . . Diana is determined to get to the truth about Alice's fate, even if she has to persuade the aloof and eminently eligible Edgar Godolphin to help her.

JASMINA SVENNE

FORGET-ME-NOT

Complete and Unabridged

LINFORD
Leicester

First published in Great Britain in 2012

First Linford Edition
published 2013

*A catalogue record for this book is available
from the British Library*

ISBN 978–1–4448–1542–9

Published by
F. A. Thorpe (Publishing)
Anstey, Leicestershire

Set by Words & Graphics Ltd.
Anstey, Leicestershire
Printed and bound in Great Britain by
T. J. International Ltd., Padstow, Cornwall

This book is printed on acid-free paper

The Long Silence

'Has the post not arrived yet?' She had resolved not to say a word, but the day had dragged in such a desultory fashion that when the maid entered to clear away the tea tray, Diana could no longer contain herself.

'No, Miss Aspley, not yet.'

'Really, Diana, you must learn to have a little patience,' her stepmother rebuked her, not even waiting for the maid to retire from the room.

Diana could not repress a sigh as she leaned back in her armchair.

'I pray you, child, do not slump like that. It is a most inelegant and unladylike habit and will do you no favours in polite society.'

'Oh, but madam, who is to see me? There's nobody here but ourselves.'

Nevertheless, Diana drew herself upright.

'*I* shall see you. And I do not wish you to cultivate habits in private that you may inadvertently repeat in public. I won't have it said that I do not take as much care of you as I would if you were my own daughter.'

It was incredibly tempting to mouth the last sentence along with the older woman, Diana had heard it so often in the past ten years.

She could have made a dozen arguments against her stepmother's pronouncement. Indeed she had often done so in the past. But it hadn't done her a scrap of good and she was not in spirits for another battle with Mrs Aspley.

Besides which, now that Papa was no longer here to stand as a screen between his only surviving child and his second wife, Diana had been trying to teach herself to be more circumspect in what she did and said, even if it went against the grain. If Mrs Aspley chose to punish her in one way or another, there was nobody to appeal to any more.

Diana bit her lip and blinked back her tears. She wouldn't cry, not now, not when Mrs Aspley would think it was her displeasure that had caused her tears. Though a glance in her direction informed Diana that the older woman was too immersed in her fine stitching to pay her any attention.

It was nearly six months since Diana's father had died. He had dropped dead of an apoplexy as he stepped out of the chaise upon their return from a shopping expedition to Nottingham, a trip Mrs Aspley had insisted upon since they were to spend Christmas with Diana's best friend and intended to pass the subsequent Season in London.

'The child must look at least halfway presentable, until we can order some proper London fashions for her,' Mrs Aspley had urged her husband before setting out. 'I won't have Mrs Simmonds and her friends saying I've neglected Diana and turned her into a dowdy, simply because she is not my daughter.'

The irony was that not one of those pretty sprigged muslin or silk gowns had seen the light of day or the inside of a ballroom or theatre, because inevitably both the house party and the London Season had been postponed for a year and Mrs Aspley and her stepdaughter had worn nothing but unrelieved black ever since.

Diana sighed, draped her sewing over the arm of her chair and wandered across to the window. She was restless and in want of a walk, even if it was only as far as the shrubbery and back. But she was almost certain her stepmother would object that it was too hot or too near to dinner time or some other trifling thing, as if Diana was not more than willing to go alone and leave the older woman to strain her eyes over her sewing.

Diana chewed her lip fretfully. Why had Alice not written? This long silence was totally out of character. Alice had written to her faithfully once a week — and sometimes more frequently than that — ever since they had left school. Even after her departure for London, her letters had continued to arrive. And now for more than a month — nothing.

'Really, Diana, must you fidget so?' Mrs Aspley asked in long-suffering tones, though without raising her eyes from her needlework. 'You are blocking the light. Do you not have something useful to occupy yourself with?'

'I'm going for a walk,' she replied abruptly.

'Diana, I do not like your tone. Come back at once.'

But Diana did not wait. Her stepmother's voice faded behind her as she hurtled out of the drawing room, along the narrow passage to the front door and out into the country lane.

Anyone would think she was still eleven instead of twenty-one from the way Mrs Aspley talked to her. Though when she had once pointed this out, her stepmother had retorted that she would stop treating her like a child when she stopped behaving like one.

It was already the middle of June and the hedgerows were full of wildflowers. But Diana barely saw them until a cluster of blue amid the grass drew her eye. Her steps slowed. She crouched and stretched her fingertips towards the tiny, sky-blue blossoms with their golden eyes.

Forget-me-nots.

'We'll always be friends, won't we?' she had whispered to Alice on that last day at school. 'No matter what happens.'

'No matter what happens,' Alice repeated, pressing the cluster of forget-me-nots into her hands.

But Diana had split the bunch, returning half the flowers to Alice. And then there had hardly been enough time left for one more embrace because Mrs Aspley's voice had interrupted them and Papa had handed her into the chaise and she had been driven away for the very last time from the school in which she had been incarcerated ever since her father's second marriage because she was — she had been told it often enough — a difficult child.

Think before you act, Diana. You are far too impetuous and daring for a girl. You cannot behave in this way. Nobody will ever marry you if you do not learn to be more ladylike.

But I don't have a bad heart, she had wanted to plead. I am not wicked by nature. I want to be good. I want . . .

Diana stopped herself. Thinking in this way about things long past would not do any good.

Still she could not help feeling abandoned. So many times in the last weeks she had opened her favourite novel, *Evelina*, in which she had pressed Alice's forget-me-nots, though the flowers were faded now and so delicate, she feared they would crumble to dust if handled too roughly. What on earth could have gone wrong? What could be so terrible that her best friend could not confide in her?

She and Alice had been inseparable since the day they had both arrived as new girls at the school.

Alice had helped Diana to behave, calming her whenever she had come close to flying into a rage over some injustice. But most of all, when they were alone, she had comforted Diana while she cried because her mother had not even been dead a year when her father had remarried, evidently feeling that his wayward and imaginative daughter needed a mother's care.

It was unfortunate that her father had chosen a woman of plain, good sense and no imagination whatsoever. Sometimes, as she grew older, Diana had even wondered whether her father too had not come to feel he had been overhasty and had made the wrong choice. The Aspley household was run with ruthless efficiency. But the joy seemed to have gone out of the house with the advent of the second Mrs Aspley.

That was why Diana had been so

looking forward to her first Season in London. Not only would there be all the excitement of seeing new places, meeting new people, wearing new clothes, but she would have been able to spend time with Alice.

Alice's letter, in reply to Diana's tear-blotted, black-bordered scrawl to explain why they would not be able to come to the house party after all, had been one of the few things that had been able to comfort her in the first dark weeks after her father's death.

I wish now that I did not have to go to London, but could come and stay with you instead, Alice had written amongst her other condolences.

Naturally Diana couldn't allow her to continue in that strain. She had written back, insisting that Alice must enjoy Christmas and the London Season for both of them and write to tell her every single insignificant detail, to distract her from the fact that she was now an orphan.

And Alice had been true to her word.

She had written about the guests her parents had invited, the gentlemen who danced and conversed with her, the entertainments she had taken part in. Diana felt as if she too had laughed at Mr Drake's witticisms or sighed over Mr Beaumont's readings of sentimental verse.

Even so, Diana had sensed a measure of restraint in Alice's letters. At the time she had assumed that Alice had not wanted to dwell too much on her happiness while her friend was still grieving. Now Diana couldn't help wondering if Alice had been harbouring her own secret sorrow — especially when Diana contrasted the London letters with those Alice had written before and during Christmas.

In her last letter in particular, there had been a hint that Alice might soon have news of some sort to impart. Initially Diana had assumed this implied that Alice might have been expecting one of her admirers to declare himself. Now she couldn't help fearing there had been something ominous about that last letter.

Could the gentleman in question have failed to propose or, still worse, had become engaged to somebody else? Was Alice heartbroken but unwilling to burden her friend while she was still in mourning? As far as affairs of the heart were concerned, Alice had always been more secretive than Diana, who had been known on occasions to admit to admiring one gentleman or another, though not even she had gone any further than that — not least because she had had so few opportunities to meet any eligible men.

But that was neither here nor there, Diana chided herself. It was the condition of Alice's heart that concerned her at present and not her own. She had written to Alice several times in the last weeks, spinning out what little news she had and trying hard not to sound reproachful at her friend's long silence, while urging her to confide in her. Alice had consoled her while she was grieving for first one parent, then the other. Now she wanted to return the favour, if only Alice would let her.

Diana shuddered in the manner said to denote someone walking over your grave. She knew she would have to go back to the house soon, to face her stepmother's wrath. But she did not really want to go.

The jingle of metal made her head whip round towards the honey-coloured sandstone house she would eventually inherit, once her stepmother, who had a life interest in it, had died. She forced herself to stare hard at the rider plodding towards her, making sure that it really was the postman and that she was not simply deceiving herself by seeing what she wanted to see.

Snatching two handfuls of petticoats, Diana began to run. It was only as she reached the door that she realised her stepmother's disapproval would be compounded if it was so glaringly obvious when she got inside that she had been running again.

She knew she ought to change her shoes, tidy her hair, maybe even wash her hands and face so she could catch her breath before she presented herself before Mrs Aspley. But what if, at last, Alice's letter had arrived? What if there was more than one? Maybe they had been delayed for some reason and would all arrive at the same time.

No, she could not wait. She burst into the drawing room, still panting, still red-cheeked and dizzy from her exertions. There was no mistake. Mrs Aspley looked up from unfastening the postbag, her gaze glacial.

'Really, Diana, you are not ten years old any more. I would have thought that in all these years, I might have left some little influence on you. Evidently I was mistaken.'

Diana bit down her instinctively rebellious response. She had to appease her stepmother. It was the only way to get what she wanted in the shortest possible time. She dropped a curtsey and tried in vain to slow her breathing.

'I'm very sorry, madam,' she said. 'It's just that I saw the postman — not that *that* is any excuse,' she amended hastily, seeing her stepmother purse her lips. 'I promise I'll try to mend my ways in the future.'

Don't ask her about the post, Diana warned herself. *Don't let her see how eager you are, it will only make her keep you waiting longer and lecture you more.*

And to her surprise, she thought she detected a slight softening in Mrs Aspley's expression.

'You have made such promises in the past,' she said, but her voice was not quite as severe as it had been.

'I know, but I really do mean it.'

'I don't lecture you for my own pleasure, you know. It is for your own good. You will never find yourself a husband if you continue to behave as you do. And though your father left you comfortably off, all of that could be easily frittered away by the first plausible villain you meet if you do not find someone to take care of your interests, like a good husband would. I shall not be here forever to look after you, you know.'

Again Diana was forced to bite her lip. She was tempted to ask why she could not learn to manage her own affairs, so that nobody would be able to take advantage of her ignorance.

But Alice's letter, if there was one in the postbag, was more important, she told herself. She dropped her eyes, pretending to be meek, rather than actually trying to peep at the handwriting on the letters in her stepmother's hands.

Perhaps she ought to try the power of silence more often, she mused. This time Mrs Aspley seemed to grumble herself to a standstill more quickly than usual. While she continued lecturing, she began to sift mechanically through the letters. One packet after another was piled up on the coffee table. Even upside down, Diana could see they were all addressed to her stepmother.

All except the very last and thickest package. Mrs Aspley stopped in the middle of a sentence, frowned, then held it out to Diana.

'For you,' she said.

'Oh, thank you, Stepmamma,' Diana said instinctively and she saw Mrs Aspley frown again. For some reason she had never liked that appellation and Diana only ever used it in moments of irritation when she wanted to provoke her stepmother. But this time it had slipped out inadvertently.

Diana frowned at the letter. It was not Alice's handwriting after all. Indeed she did not think she recognised this firm, masculine hand. What's more, she knew her stepmother was thinking precisely the same thing. She would expect Diana to show her the letter once she had read it, or at very least to tell her who it was from and what it was all about.

With a sense of foreboding, Diana broke the seal of the covering sheet. As she unfolded it, several more letters that had been enclosed in it spilled out into her lap. One even slipped and fell to the floor. She stooped to pick it up.

The handwriting on this letter was all too familiar, as was the address and the seal with which it was fastened. With growing fear, Diana sifted through all the other sealed letters in her lap. All written in her own handwriting, all addressed to Alice, all unopened.

Only the reverse of the covering sheet bore a few lines of the other, alien handwriting. As her eyes skimmed the words in growing disbelief, Diana uttered an inarticulate cry.

'What is it, child?'

Diana could not reply. Her eyes were passing over and over those scrawled words, trying to wrest a different meaning from them.

Dear Miss Aspley

I regret to inform you that our daughter, Alice, is recently deceased.

I take the liberty of returning your letters in the belief that that is what our daughter would have wished.

Your obedient servant,
Geo. Simmonds

An Eligible Bachelor

'You will be on your best behaviour, won't you, Diana? I shall *die* of mortification if you should start any of your tricks. Mr Godolphin is such an eligible bachelor, half of London is desperate to ensnare him, and first impressions are so important . . . '

Diana hardly even heard her stepmother, though she could not quite ignore her fussing as Mrs Aspley flitted round her, now tugging at the artful folds of her sprigged muslin gown; now rearranging the dark ringlets that clustered around Diana's neck.

The image in the mirror before which she stood bore little resemblance to the black-clad figure with hair neatly swept back that Diana had grown used to. Nearly a year had passed since Alice's death and Diana at last found herself in London, in a house her stepmother had

19

taken for the Season.

On the one hand, Diana had been looking forward to escaping from enforced isolation in which Mrs Aspley was her only permanent companion. But being here, without her father, without her best friend, was going to be a bittersweet experience.

She hadn't been able to stop thinking about Alice during the past weeks of preparation and throughout the journey hither, particularly when Mrs Aspley, bored by the scenery and exhausted after expatiating on all her plans for Diana, had finally fallen into an uneasy doze.

Diana knew there was some mystery connected with Alice's death because she had not been able to glean any more details about it. Nobody could or would tell her how her friend had died or when or even where she was buried.

She had written a letter of sympathy to Alice's parents, hinting that she would have liked to know more, but received no reply. She had scoured the newspapers for an announcement of Alice's death, however brief, which might give her some clue. But she had found nothing.

She wished she had some mutual acquaintance with the Simmonds whom she could ask. But Alice's family came from Leicestershire and Diana knew nobody there. Nor had she remained in contact with any of the other girls they had been at school with and she had no reason to believe any of them would have been better informed about the manner of Alice's death than she was herself.

There was only one other person she could turn to — and that was her stepmother. On the day that Mr Simmonds's letter arrived, Mrs Aspley had been awkwardly sympathetic. Diana had even thought that, in time, they might have grown closer as a result.

But it was not to be. Just a few weeks after Diana learned of Alice's death, another letter had arrived, this one from London and addressed to Mrs

Aspley. Diana gathered it was from some old friend of her stepmother, to whom she had apparently appealed for gossip about Alice Simmonds on Diana's behalf. But when Diana tried to discover what news the letter contained, Mrs Aspley had grown icily cold again.

'You are *never* to speak that name again, or to ask me any more questions about her,' she said. 'I find I have been very remiss in allowing you to keep up a correspondence with such a pernicious influence — heaven knows what would have happened if you had met up again in London. I suppose we should be grateful that you have not been seen in public with her since leaving school.'

Diana had been so stunned by this tirade, she could barely utter a word at first. *She* had always been deemed to be a bad influence on Alice, and not the other way round.

'But why? What's happened? What has she done? How did she die?'

But not another word would Mrs

Aspley utter on the subject. She only grew angrier the more Diana persisted and threatened to withhold her step-daughter's allowance and refuse all invitations if her injunctions were not obeyed.

But just because she never spoke of Alice, it did not mean Diana thought about her less. She had even considered trying to find that fatal letter, to discover the worst for herself.

It was even possible that Mrs Aspley had burnt the letter because one day during that unhappy period, on returning home from a walk, Diana had noticed some charred fragments of paper on the hearth, even though it was too warm a day for a fire to be necessary.

She had turned the dilemma over and over in her mind and the only explanation she could find that would fit the circumstances was if Alice had died by her own hand as a result of being disappointed in love. And if that was the case, Diana could not shake her feelings of guilt that she had not tried harder to persuade her friend to confide in her.

'Diana? Diana!' A sharp voice interrupted her brooding. 'I declare, you have not been listening to a word I've said. Sometimes I don't know why I even bother to give you these opportunities when it would be far less trouble for me to stay at home and let you become an old maid.'

The thought of returning to the dreariness of home forced Diana to make an effort.

'I'm very sorry. I was just thinking about — about Papa.' She barely managed to catch herself in time before she blurted out the truth.

Mrs Aspley pursed her lips and her sharp eyes scrutinised her stepdaughter's face, as if assessing if she was telling the truth. Diana felt a flash of resentment. A loving wife would have looked tearful at having the memory of her dead husband evoked like this.

You didn't love Papa any more than

you love me, she whispered silently, and then wondered whether she really wanted to be loved by this woman, whose charge she was obliged to be.

Perhaps it would not be so bad to be married and escape to a new home. Maybe they would both be happier if they were not forced to live together as they were. Which meant she would do well to listen to her stepmother because Diana had absolutely no doubt that Mrs Aspley knew what would or would not repel any potential suitors, since her advice tallied with that of every novel, conduct book or sermon Diana had ever read.

But just then a carriage came to a rattling halt in front of the house and Mrs Aspley scurried to the window in a way she would have deplored if Diana had done it.

'Oh, they're here, they're here,' she gasped, suddenly in a flutter and fanning herself with her handkerchief. 'You *will* behave, won't you?'

Diana stole another glance at Edgar Godolphin out of the corner of her eye. She disliked admitting that her step-mother was right about anything, but there was no denying the gentleman sitting beside her in the hackney coach was extremely good looking.

Otherwise she had had very little opportunity to judge what this much-vaunted 'eligible bachelor' was really like. On being introduced to her, Mr Godolphin had pressed her hand briefly in his firm, cool grip, inclined his body in a polite bow and uttered the utterly conventional and utterly meaningless, 'Delighted to make your acquaintance.'

Though to be fair, he had not had a chance to say much more than that before they were all swept up by the whirlwind that was his mother.

'Well, well, come along now. No time to waste,' Mrs Godolphin exclaimed with a comical smile. 'The sooner we get to the Foundling Hospital, the sooner we can show off our finery and our charitable dispositions.'

Diana had not expected to like Mrs Godolphin, for no better reason than because she was an old acquaintance of her stepmother. But she had been pleasantly surprised when they had met the previous evening at a private concert.

Mrs Godolphin had greeted Diana with a cheerful, 'Ah, so this is the pretty stepdaughter I've heard so much about.'

Moreover there had been numerous occasions during that first meeting when Diana had felt Mrs Godolphin was closer to her in age than she was to Mrs Aspley. Since this was Diana's first visit to London, the conversation had turned inevitably to what was worth seeing in the capital. Amongst other things, Mrs Godolphin mentioned the exhibition of fine art at the Foundling Hospital.

'Such a worthwhile cause,' she added with a mischievous smile.

'Yes, indeed,' Mrs Aspley agreed in all seriousness, not to be outdone.

'You really must come with us tomorrow. My son, Edgar, has promised to escort me. Unless you have a previous engagement?'

They had not — and even if they had, Diana formed the impression that her stepmother would have excused herself from it in order to attend the Godolphins.

The Foundling Hospital was situated on the northern edge of London, as close as practical to the fresh country air. Since she was travelling backwards, Diana's first impression was of the imposing double gates, flanked by narrower arched entrances for pedestrians. Clusters of fashionably dressed people were already strolling about, enjoying the air.

It was only after the coach had stopped and she was waiting for the older ladies to be helped out that Diana managed to glimpse the main building itself. It proved to be an imposing edifice with symmetrical wings stretching a good way towards the driveway.

'Miss Aspley.'

Diana started at the sound of her name. Both older ladies had clambered out and Mr Godolphin was waiting, a shade impatiently, by the door, his hand extended towards her.

'I'm sorry,' Diana murmured and wondered vaguely if this was a serious enough trespass to earn her a scolding from her stepmother when they got back to their lodgings.

To try to compensate for her delay, Diana rushed her descent and stumbled as a result. Strong masculine fingers gripped her upper arm to steady her and she looked up into Edgar Godolphin's cool grey-green eyes.

'Really, Diana!' Mrs Aspley said with a heartfelt sigh and a shake of the head.

'I'm sorry,' Diana muttered again.

'Nonsense, it could happen to anyone,' Mrs Godolphin intervened. 'Why, I remember I almost tripped up over my hoop when I was presented to

Queen Charlotte on the occasion of my marriage . . . '

She swept the others along in her wake. Soon enough, Diana was feeling a little dizzy and overwhelmed by all there was to see — the chapel in which Mr Handel had directed annual performances of *The Messiah* until his death; the prominently placed portrait by Hogarth of Thomas Coram, the founder of the hospital; the gardens in which the boys were taught to grow fruit, vegetables and flowers to qualify them as gardeners' boys when they left; the foundlings themselves, neatly dressed in their brown serge uniforms with red trimmings and, of course, the art exhibition they had come to see.

Throughout Mrs Godolphin remained the chattering centre of their party. Both Diana and Mrs Aspley were drawn in and it was only when she turned away from a portrait of a family group that Diana caught sight of Edgar Godolphin and realised he had hardly spoken a word. She frowned slightly, and then blushed as he turned his head unexpectedly and caught her contemplating his face.

'You appear to be looking in the wrong direction, Miss Aspley,' he said in neutral tones. 'The pictures are on the walls.'

His expression was as unreadable as his voice, but the twinkle in his eye betrayed him.

Diana curtsied in reply.

'Thank you very much, sir,' she replied. 'I would never have found them without your assistance.'

A smile broke the serenity of his expression and Mrs Godolphin laughed aloud.

'Well, Edgar, it seems you have met your match,' she said and seemed not to notice, as Diana did, that her son suddenly stiffened and the smile faded from his lips.

Throughout the remainder of their visit, he devoted himself to Mrs Aspley, asking her opinion on the various portraits, landscapes and allegorical paintings on display.

Eventually the time came to return to their lodgings to dress for dinner. The traffic was so heavy, the coach came to a halt about halfway back, but the delay was a matter of indifference to Diana. She was still sifting the impressions of the day as her gaze flitted idly from one passer-by to the next.

At length her eyes fixed upon one figure in particular. Amidst the bustle, she alone was motionless, her head bowed over a bundle tucked into the crook of her arm. Diana had time to notice that the cut of the stranger's pelisse was good, though it and the gown she wore beneath had grown shabby from frequent wear, the hems stained with mud.

Afterwards it seemed to Diana that everything happened at once. Perhaps the woman sensed her gaze. At any rate, she turned and looked straight up at Diana. The conversation in the hackney coach, the complaints of Mrs Aspley about the delay, receded into a background hiss, like distant waves, as Diana found herself gazing deep into a pair of large, blue eyes.

The stare seemed to last an infinity. Diana felt her thoughts whirl and shift and change pattern, like leaves on an autumnal wind. A thousand things she should have understood before suddenly made sense. The revelation paralysed her. But she knew she could not be mistaken.

It was the other woman who broke the spell. She backed away, still staring at Diana, and bumped against another passer-by. That one check was apparently enough. She tore her gaze away from Diana, turned and began to push through the crowd.

At the same instant, Diana darted forward, groping to unfasten the door of the coach.

'Alice!' she cried out.

A Baby's Cry

Diana was vaguely aware of a bustle and stir amongst her fellow passengers at her cry. But she had no time to think about them or propriety or anything else. Her only thought was that she could not let Alice disappear again. She had to understand what had happened, what had gone wrong.

The door clattered open. She felt a restraining hand grab her arm as she started forward, but she wrenched herself free. Something caught and ripped, but she was past caring. The drop down to the pavement was steep without the aid of the steps. She felt a jarring sensation through her feet as she landed on the paving slabs, but she forced herself to run in the direction in which Alice had disappeared.

From the elevation of the hackney coach she had been able to see Alice's hat clearly amidst the throng, but now she felt dwarfed and insignificant, swimming blindly through a sea of strangers. The thin wail of an infant caught her ear and she remembered for the first time the unmistakable bundle Alice had been carrying in her arms.

Diana remembered again how thin and pale Alice had looked. She was not well. She was undernourished.

Diana was not used to running any more, having given up such hoydenish ways on the day she was told Alice had died. Her heart was beating against her ribs, her lungs squeezed by the stiffness of her stays. Just a little further, just a little further. The baby's cries lured her on like a siren's song.

She faltered as she reached some crossroads and peered in every direction for any sign of Alice's hat or holly green pelisse. Nothing. And then she heard it again. A hiccup and a gurgle and then the baby's wails louder, closer than ever.

With renewed confidence Diana

followed the sound, though it troubled her that she could see no sign of a young mother with a child. A narrow alley between two rows of shops opened up before her eyes. She ran towards its entrance eagerly and stumbled to a standstill.

There in the gloom, a young woman was crouched on the edge of a shallow step leading to a side entrance to the soot-blackened building. A small hand flailed weakly, scrabbling at the young mother's tattered bodice.

The girl glanced up at Diana with the eyes of a world-weary crone.

'Spare a penny, Miss?' she rasped in a hollow, hopeless tone, as if by instinct alone. As if the words had been said so often, they had ceased to have any meaning.

As soon as Diana had realised it was not Alice, she had turned away and closed her eyes. But the girl's heart-rending appeal roused her. She groped automatically for her purse. Still struggling for breath, she hesitated over a shilling, but seeing the girl's ragged state, it seemed so pathetically little, she changed it for half a crown.

How much have we spent in the last days on coach fares and concert tickets alone?

'Why don't you come with me?' Diana blurted out impulsively. 'I'll make sure you get a decent feed and give you a cast-off gown and . . . '

The astonishment in the girl's eyes as she lifted her head made Diana falter. What was she thinking? What would her stepmother say if she returned to the hackney coach with this ragged waif in tow? And she was not at all sure if the presence of the Godolphins would make the situation better or worse.

But the sight of her open purse, the glint of silver had attracted other, unwanted attention. She had not noticed any other beggars before this. Indeed, she had not noticed anyone apart from the waif and her baby. But now, as if smelling wealth, they seemed to appear everywhere.

That was the first time Diana began to grow frightened. She was alone in a street she did not know in a city with which she was barely familiar and then only the more salubrious parts. Her presence here, alone, could be misinterpreted. She did not know how these people lived.

She could give them every penny she owned and still it would not be enough. And then how would she manage all those weeks in London that still lay ahead, without money for emergencies? She knew her stepmother would not give her an advance on her allowance if she overstretched herself so recklessly.

There was no time to stop and think. By instinct she turned back the way she had come and walked on rapidly, her head lowered, her fingers still plucking nervously at her purse in an agony of indecision, hoping they would all drop away and leave her alone.

The waif and her baby haunted her. Could she have been mistaken about the figure she had followed? Perhaps it had not been Alice at all. How likely was it that someone from such a good home, with such respectable parents, should end up like this?

But if it wasn't Alice, why had she run? Did she think I was someone else? Did she think I meant to harm her or her baby?

Diana's steps wavered. Was this really the way she had come? She could not remember passing that pawnbroker's shop with all those clothes hanging in the window, or that cook-shop from which savoury smells were emanating.

'Three little 'uns starving at home.' The words made Diana jump and she looked round into the ravaged face of a woman limping persistently alongside her. 'Had a daughter, much like yourself, bless your pretty face, till she took sick and died and left me to take care of the little 'uns . . . '

There was something hard about the woman's eyes, but Diana knew that did not necessarily mean she was lying. Hardship could have aged her, given her that blank gaze, as if she was past caring about anything any more.

She fumbled with the drawstrings of her purse, wondering if she dared ask the woman for directions. But directions to where? She had no idea what the street was called in which the hackney coach had been trapped by the traffic.

'Miss Aspley.'

She started so violently that the shilling fell out of her hand. Instantly the crone bent to retrieve it, but a swifter urchin got to it first.

'Oh, Mr Godolphin,' Diana gasped.

It didn't matter that she barely knew him or that an extremely grim frown darkened his brow. The relief at seeing a familiar face made her want to fling her arms about his neck.

But the beggar-woman was screeching abuse at the thieving ragamuffin as he dodged his way into the throng. Diana turned towards her, shocked at those words she understood — and some she had never heard before but which she assumed must be rude — but also feeling guilty at her carelessness and wanting to make amends.

Mr Godolphin shared none of her qualms.

'Come along,' he said irritably, snatching her hand and forcibly tucking it through the crook of his elbow. 'And for heaven's sake, put away that purse, unless you want to be fleeced by every vagabond in the area.'

'Oh, but, sir, you don't understand. I . . .'

He began to stride away rapidly, yanking her along with him so she was forced to trot in an attempt to keep up with him.

'Do you have any idea how much danger you might have put yourself in?' Mr Godolphin demanded in a low, angry tone. 'Not to mention what a nuisance you have made of yourself. Mrs Aspley was almost in hysterics when I left her and I have better things to do with my time than to pursue runaways.'

'I'm very sorry, sir.'

It was on the tip of Diana's tongue to explain about Alice, but something held her back. Partly it was because she scarcely knew Edgar Godolphin and he was so obviously angry. But more than anything, she realised, it was because if what she had seen was true, if it really had been Alice, then she wanted to protect her friend for as long as possible from public exposure. Mr Godolphin had never met Alice. He wouldn't understand.

No, the person she had to talk to was her stepmother. She alone could clarify the confusion in Diana's mind, tell her the truth about her friend if, as she suspected, both Mr Simmonds and Mrs Aspley had lied to her about Alice's fate.

As it was, she did not have enough breath to defend herself and keep up the relentless pace Mr Godolphin set. But she was too proud to ask him to slow down.

Never had she been more pleased to

see her stepmother peering out of the hackney coach. But her relief was short-lived. Even before she had managed to clamber inside, Mrs Aspley had already begun to berate her for her inexcusable behaviour. Even Mrs Godolphin looked uncomfortable, though she made an attempt to deflect Mrs Aspley's wrath away from her charge.

'I'm sure there is a perfectly reasonable explanation for everything,' she said, but her smile was uncertain, as if she could think of no suitable excuse and was afraid Diana would not be able to find one either.

'I thought I saw somebody I knew,' Diana said. 'I wanted to talk to her . . .'

'Yes, well, that's quite enough of that,' Mrs Aspley intervened brusquely and Diana realised her stepmother was terrified that she might blurt out too much in the presence of the Godolphins about the undesirable acquaintances she had formed in the past.

* * *

'I don't know how you can embarrass me so in front of the Godolphins and put yourself in such danger. Anything might have happened to you. Heaven knows what the Godolphins will tell all their influential friends about you. This reflects badly upon me too, you know.'

The front door had barely closed behind them before Mrs Aspley burst forth with all her accumulated grievances.

Diana pushed aside the memory of her fear when she had realised she was alone and lost in an alien city, because she didn't want to acknowledge that her stepmother had made a fair point. There were other more pressing matters to deal with.

'Why didn't you tell me the truth about Alice Simmonds?' Diana demanded.

Mrs Aspley turned puce at this allegation.

'Are you accusing me of *lying*?' she

blustered, but Diana thought she caught a glimpse of fear in her stepmother's eyes. 'If your father was alive . . . '

'Well, he isn't, but Alice is,' Diana cut her stepmother short. 'I saw her in the street. That's why I ran off like that.'

Her voice wavered slightly. Was she absolutely certain it was Alice she had seen? Could she have been mistaken?

'That's impossible. Alice Simmonds is dead. Her own father wrote to tell you so.'

But there was something odd about the way Mrs Aspley was pacing restlessly about the room, picking up and putting down an ornament, a letter opener, a fire screen, as if she did not dare meet her stepdaughter's eye. Diana was more convinced than ever that she was lying.

'I know what I saw,' she persisted stubbornly. 'She was shabbily dressed and carrying a baby, but I know it was her. She looked me straight in the eyes.'

Diana stuck out her chin defiantly

and she had the satisfaction of seeing Mrs Aspley flinch at her revelations.

'Oh no, she grows worse and worse,' she muttered to herself.

'I know you found out something more about Alice from your friend. I know because you'd always talked of Alice kindly before and then suddenly I wasn't even allowed to mention her name. Don't I deserve to know the fate of my best friend?' Diana tried to soften her tone, hoping that wheedling would be more effective than confrontation.

'Oh, for heaven's sake, you would try the patience of a saint.'

'And if you won't tell me, then I suppose I shall have to write to Alice's parents again.'

Now at last Mrs Aspley turned her glare upon Diana's face.

'You wouldn't dare. I forbid it.'

'What other choice have you left me?'

Diana let the words hang in the sudden silence of the drawing room. She could see her stepmother struggling with contradictory emotions.

'Oh, very well,' she snapped at last. 'Your precious Alice ran away from home when her parents discovered she was carrying a child out of wedlock — the result of an unfortunate entanglement formed during that ill-fated house party, which thankfully we could not attend. Now are you satisfied? And you needn't ask me any more questions because that's all I know.'

Diana sat down abruptly on the couch. Somewhere at the back of her mind, she had known from the first moment she caught sight of Alice that this could be the only explanation. But still she felt it as a physical blow. She had not wanted it to be true. She had wanted some other explanation, per-haps that Alice had eloped with someone her parents disapproved of and that she was now an impoverished but respectable wife. Or that Alice had been forced, for whatever reason, to take a position caring for somebody else's baby.

But just because Alice has lapsed from virtue, it doesn't mean I should abandon her, Diana told herself. Indeed, the more friendless Alice was, the more she needed help. And they had promised to be friends forever, no matter what happened.

'We must find her,' Diana mused and was startled by the sound of her own voice. She hadn't intended to utter those words aloud.

'Over my dead body. This is precisely why I did not want to tell you because I knew you would want to begin one of your crusades and ruin your reputation and your marriage prospects into the bargain. Do you have any idea what people will say about you if you are known to be consorting with a woman of that type?'

Diana saw red.

'How can you talk that way?' she cried, jumping to her feet. 'Alice is *not* that type of woman. You *know* she must have been deceived by some unscrupulous rake who took advantage of her kind heart and trusting nature. And anyway she's my friend and we promised . . . '

'Yes, yes, I know all about your girlish nonsense.' Mrs Aspley dismissed her words with a wave of her hand. 'But nobody ever keeps those silly promises. It's high time you grew up, Diana. Now I do not want to hear another word on the subject. Is that understood?'

'But . . . '

'I mean it, Diana. Not another word, or I will take you straight home again, out of harm's way.'

Diana did not reply. But if her stepmother had seen the mutinous look on her face as she turned away to go and dress for dinner, she would have known the subject was far from over.

A Plan Is Set

'You are absolutely certain you won't change your mind?' Mrs Aspley asked one last time as she tugged on her gloves.

Diana replied with no more than an exasperated look.

'Very well then, have it your own way.'

Mrs Aspley shrugged and swept out of the drawing room, in all likelihood pleased enough to have some time to herself. Diana heaved a sigh of relief as the door closed behind her.

The atmosphere in the Aspley household had been strained since the previous evening. Diana had accompanied her stepmother to a dinner party to which they had both been invited, but she had barely spoken or heard a word all night. Instead she had been turning over one plan after another until she found the only one she thought had even the remotest chance of being carried out successfully.

With this in mind, she had declined to accompany her stepmother on a shopping expedition to Oxford Street, claiming to have a headache. No doubt Mrs Aspley thought she was sulking and that missing the trip would be a salutary lesson, but Diana didn't have time to dwell on such irrelevancies.

As soon as the front door closed behind her stepmother, she took herself up to her bedroom, just in case Mrs Aspley returned before she had finished what she intended to do. And if Mrs Aspley asked the servants what her stepdaughter had been doing in her absence, they would be able to tell her quite truthfully that she had sequestered herself as if she really was ill. It wasn't strictly a lie, Diana told herself, because, due to a sleepless night, her head was stinging, particularly behind the eyes.

But there was a job to be done and

she did not know when else she would get another opportunity. So she unlocked her writing desk, found a clean sheet of paper, trimmed the nib of her quill and opened the inkwell.

As girls, she and Alice had often pored over any newspapers that came their way, looking for unusual advertisements. There were families asking for information about a relative who was believed to have eloped or been abducted. There were wealthy widows appealing for second husbands, or confirmed bachelors looking for a wife in order to spite over-presumptuous heirs apparent. There were even young gentlemen declaring their undying admiration for a beautiful young lady glimpsed only once from a distance at the opera or riding through Hyde Park.

Diana hoped their old interest in advertisements might make Alice scan them for old times' sake, so she would see the one Diana intended to place.

But it was, she found, one thing to have a plan and quite another to carry it out. All night, elaborate phrases and sentences had drifted through her head, but now most of them seemed to have disappeared and she could not seem to get those that remained in the right order.

It took several drafts and a good deal of ink before Diana achieved something she was at least half satisfied with. She had even taken the precaution of smuggling a copy of *The Times* upstairs, so she could copy out the address. But when she came to seal the letter, she could find no sealing wax in her disorganised desk, though she was almost certain she must have some.

Diana compressed her lips. She hadn't come all this way to be thwarted at the last hurdle. She knew her stepmother had some sealing wax downstairs in the library. She could have rung for one of the servants to fetch it, but then they would have known she had been writing letters rather than lying down and nursing her head.

No, there was only one thing she could do. She would steal down to the library, seal the letter there and bribe one of the maids to post it without her stepmother's knowledge.

Fortune seemed to favour Diana. She did not meet any of the servants on her way down, though she heard them working behind closed doors. Either they were too busy to hear her steps on the creaking stairs, or else they mistook her for just another servant going about her business.

At any rate she reached the library without meeting a soul. It took a little time, however, to locate a stick of red wax and it had still not melted when Diana heard a smart rap at the outer door.

She held her breath as a nearby maid opened the door.

'I'm sorry, sir, Mrs Aspley is not at home and Miss Aspley is lying down with a headache,' she heard the maid reply.

Diana let out a sigh of relief. She had

been irrationally afraid her stepmother had returned earlier than she had anticipated and would catch her out, even though Mrs Aspley rarely had any business in the library.

Diana was vaguely aware that the voices, the maid's and the deeper voice evidently belonging to the gentleman caller, continued to speak in the hall, but she turned her attention instead to dripping a pool of red wax on the correct spot where the two edges of the covering sheet met and then pressing her seal into the molten wax.

'Expected home soon, sir . . . '

'I'll wait if I may . . . '

'Certainly, sir.'

Diana picked out a few stray words without taking in their meaning, until the maid continued.

'Perhaps you'd care to step into the library?'

Diana nearly cried out in dismay. She threw a hasty look round the room, but there was only one door. The only other means of escaping undetected would have been through the tall sash windows and, since she could hear the maid's hand on the doorknob, she knew she had not enough time to reach the nearest window, let alone open it, scramble out, close it as best she could and scuttle out of sight.

No, there was no way out of it. She would have to receive her stepmother's guest as graciously as she could and claim that her headache had improved so far that she had thought a book might pass her time.

The maid did not enter the room, merely opening the door for the visitor before withdrawing and closing the door behind her. Since he was looking straight ahead, the caller did not spot Diana immediately.

She started as she recognised him and the letter fell out from between her nerveless fingers. It landed with a light slap on the carpet and the gentleman snapped his head round in the direction of the unexpected sound. It was Edgar Godolphin.

Though he must have been the more surprised of the pair, Mr Godolphin was the first to move. Diana also darted forward, but she was too late. The visitor had already retrieved her letter and was straightening up from his stooped position.

'Thank you, sir,' Diana murmured, curtseying, though she was flustered at the unusual position she found herself in, alone with a gentleman she barely knew and with no chaperone in sight.

But Mr Godolphin's gaze had frozen on the address on the letter in his hand and Diana's heart began to beat faster. She held out her hand, but instead of passing the letter back to her, Mr Godolphin fixed one of his sternest looks upon her face.

'Why the devil are you writing to a newspaper?'

He made no apology for his choice of language and Diana raised her chin a little higher.

'I don't see that that is any business of yours,' she retorted haughtily.

'Maybe not, but I *am* a friend of the family. Or would you rather I asked your mother?'

'No!' The word came out as sharply as a bird's alarm call. 'And she isn't my mother, she's my stepmother.'

Mr Godolphin shrugged lightly.

'Mother or stepmother, she is still responsible for your welfare until you are married,' he said. 'So which is it to be? Are you going to trust me with the truth, or should I give this,' he flourished the letter before her eyes, 'to Mrs Aspley when she returns?'

Diana flushed. It was an impossible situation. She knew her stepmother would disapprove of her course of action, but to be forced to confide in this man of all people, after the previous day's events, was galling in the extreme. She was under no delusions that he either liked or approved of her.

'I — I want to find a friend,' Diana blurted out the words against her better judgement. 'I thought perhaps an advertisement . . . '

It was clear from Mr Godolphin's expression that he was more baffled than enlightened by her explanation.

'I don't understand. Surely you know the whereabouts of your friend, or have mutual friends who might supply you with an address if it has changed or been mislaid. Unless, of course, this *friend* — ' he placed sarcastic emphasis on the word, 'is someone your family disapproves of?'

This was so close to the truth that Diana found herself reddening still further.

'Alice and I swore we would always be friends. I can't abandon her now that . . . ' Her voice caught. She still was not sure how much of the truth she ought to trust him with.

He was watching her sceptically, still keeping hold of the incriminating letter.

'They told me she was dead.' The words escaped Diana before she could stop them. Tears prickled at the back of her eyes, but fiercely she blinked them back. 'I grieved for her and then

59

yesterday I saw her in the street.'
Somehow she couldn't bring herself to
tell him about the baby or about how
threadbare Alice's clothes had grown.

'That's why you ran off like a mad
thing,' Mr Godolphin replied, keeping
his tone flat and neutral.

'Yes,' Diana admitted. She averted
her face to hide her tears, but even so
she was forced to dab at the corners of
her eyes to bring herself under control.

'But are you certain it was her? If
your friend is dead . . . '

'It was her. I know it. I asked Mrs
Aspley. She admitted they had lied to
me, thinking it was for the best.' She
pulled herself up short. If she told Mr
Godolphin that her stepmother disapproved of her wish to find Alice and
save her from destitution, he might well
take Mrs Aspley's side.

'I think you'd better tell me the
whole story,' Mr Godolphin said,
gesturing towards two comfortable
chairs.

And so she told him about her

friendship with Alice, about her supposed death, even, eventually, about the baby. She had half-expected a barrage of disapproval or criticism. Instead, he listened patiently, barely making any comments and only asking the occasional question to clarify some point.

'I see,' he said when Diana had faltered to a close. 'And what do you intend to do after you find her? Clearly your mother would disapprove of having her here and though there is a possibility you might be able to reconcile Miss Simmonds with her parents, it is not a wager I would care to stake much money on.'

Diana looked down at her hands, which were clasped tightly in her lap. She knew he was right, but she couldn't quite give up the quest, not now she had proceeded this far.

'I don't know,' she admitted in a small voice. 'I just know I can't desert her.'

There was a long silence. She felt the force of Mr Godolphin's gaze on her lowered forehead.

'Well,' he said, suddenly sounding brisk, 'I suppose there is still time to make plans if and when we find your friend.'

Diana's head whipped upward at the sound of a seal cracking. She drew in a sharp breath and reached out to try to snatch her letter out of Mr Godolphin's grasp. But he anticipated her move and was instantly on his feet.

'You've no right to read that,' she cried out, all her previous mistrust coming to the fore once more.

'Oh, come now, this is intended for public consumption. If I do not read it now, I'll be able to read it in the newspaper in a day or two, and by then it will be too late for me to excise anything that had far better have been kept private.'

His brows had drawn together into a frown. Once or twice his lips twitched, but she could not be sure if it was a smile or a sharp word that he repressed.

'Yes, well, if you wanted to attract

every fortune-hunter and confidence trickster in London, you could not have gone a better way about it,' he said.

'I beg your pardon?'

'By giving this address as the one to which correspondents should send their responses, you might as well have announced to the world how much money your family is worth.'

'I didn't know how else to manage it,' Diana stammered, because she had known it would bring her into conflict with her stepmother if the latter found any mysterious letters amongst the post. 'I know other people give the addresses of shops and inns, but . . . '

'Hmm, well, I think I can help you with that,' Mr Godolphin cut her short. 'But you also give away too many details. You must always hold something in reserve, something that nobody apart from the real Miss Simmonds would know and could tell any emissary who comes to you.'

'I assumed Alice would respond in person to the advertisement,' Diana faltered, but her companion shook his head.

'It's far more likely that you will be accosted by all sorts of impostors, claiming to be her landlord or her neighbour or a benefactor of one kind or another, in the hopes that you will open your purse to them as freely as you did yesterday in exchange for some spurious piece of information.'

'Oh.' Diana sank down into her seat, despondent.

A moment later she uttered a gasp and sprang up again as Mr Godolphin ripped the letter into fragments. As she darted forward, intent on rescuing what she could, he scattered the snowfall of paper into the fire.

'Fetch me some paper and ink,' he said. 'I see we shall have to work on this together, if you are not to be fleeced.'

For a moment Diana could not speak, hardly daring to believe she had understood him correctly.

'Do you really mean that?' she asked.

'I do. As long as you accept one condition.'

'And what might that be?' she asked, forcing herself to sound suspicious.

'That you allow me to read any replies you may receive, let me accompany you to any rendezvous that may be arranged and will at least listen to my opinions on anything you might discover, even if you reject my advice in the end.'

Part of Diana wanted to refuse indignantly and assert her independence. And yet, another part was secretly relieved that she was not alone, that there was someone older, more experienced and physically stronger than her to defend and advise her, if the need arose. If she wanted to find Alice, surely she should not be too proud to accept help?

'Very well,' she said, though the words stuck in her throat. 'There should be some writing materials in here, I think.'

An Unexpected Ally

It was an unnerving experience to have to write to Mr Godolphin's dictation while he prowled back and forth behind her chair with the suppressed energy of a caged tiger.

Twice he stopped behind her chair, his hand resting on its back so he could re-read the letter over her shoulder. At such moments she was acutely aware of his towering presence, the warmth of his breath in her hair, his fingers only a fraction of an inch from her shoulder.

She couldn't help feeling a grudging respect for him. The whole process took a lot less time than her original letter and he seemed to know exactly how to phrase things. Moreover he remembered most of the pertinent facts she had told him, only occasionally asking her to confirm or clarify some detail.

When it was done, Mr Godolphin

leaned over her shoulder one last time to pick up the letter in order to skim through it.

'Well, I think that will serve the purpose,' he said.

'But you didn't even mention Alice's baby,' Diana objected.

Mr Godolphin gave her a dry look.

'Do you want to be inundated with offers of unwanted babies from impostors, claiming the unfortunate mother died before the advertisement could appear in the paper and hinting that we might wish to contribute something to the funeral costs as well as the upkeep of the child?'

'No, I suppose not.'

Diana had the impression Mr Godolphin intended to say something more, but he raised his head sharply at the sound of a carriage drawing up in front of the house.

'Do you suppose that is your mother returning?' he asked instead.

'*Stepmother*,' Diana retorted, irritated because they had been caught off guard like this. 'Why do you find it so difficult to remember that my mother is dead?'

Mr Godolphin looked startled by her sudden vehemence. Then he reddened, as did she. What had possessed her to snap at him like that, particularly when he had undertaken to help her in her quest?

'I'm sorry. I shouldn't have . . . ' They both uttered the same words and both stopped before their sentences could diverge in different directions.

'There's no time to waste,' Mr Godolphin said briskly. 'I'll seal this and post it after I leave, if you'll put away the writing materials.'

Diana did as she was bid while her companion folded the letter and tucked it into his coat pocket. She heard the front door open and then the unmistakable sound of her stepmother's voice.

For the first time since Edgar Godolphin had stumbled across her in the library, Diana found herself wondering what Mrs Aspley would think if she realised her stepdaughter had been alone and unchaperoned with an eligible bachelor for at least half an hour. Would she purse her lips and cluck in disapproval? Or would she grow over-excited at the thought that Diana might snare such an excellent catch and become embarrassingly obvious in her matchmaking?

But Edgar Godolphin took matters into his own hands. He grabbed her by one arm and pressed the forefinger of his other hand to her lips when she uttered a gasp. Before Diana was fully aware of what he intended to do, he had bundled her against the wall and pulled the door open so she was concealed behind it.

'Ah, Mrs Aspley, I thought I heard you returning,' Mr Godolphin said. 'I believe you wished to speak to me about a matter of some importance concerning your late husband's investments?'

'Oh, Mr Godolphin, I am *so* sorry to have kept you waiting. I had no idea you would come so promptly. Please, do step into the drawing room. I cannot apologise enough.'

Her voice faded away as their steps retreated upstairs to the drawing room floor. Once the coast was clear, Diana knew she ought to creep back up the stairs, past the drawing room to the safety of her bedroom, but as was usual for her when anything dramatic had happened, she felt restless.

She had wandered across to the window of the library, to gaze blindly at the garden in the square. She was not sure how long the motionless figure had been there. But the sensation of being watched overwhelmed her. She started and her eyes seemed to be drawn inevitably to that one poorly-dressed figure, whose fist was clenching and unclenching round one of the railings in front of the house, as if she, it was a woman, could not resolve whether to venture forward and knock at the door, or if she should beat a hasty retreat.

Diana's heart leapt into her mouth,

the uncontrollable but unrealistic hope springing into her heart, as if just by thinking about Alice, she might have conjured her up.

But it was not Alice. It was the old crone Diana had encountered the previous day, the one who claimed to have three starving grandchildren at home, the sole legacy of a dead daughter. Moreover, it was obvious that the woman had seen her standing by the window. She was staring at Diana as if the force of her gaze could have drawn her outside to talk to her.

Diana pulled back, feeling as if she had been scalded. Her instinct was to run away. The thought that the woman had taken the trouble to seek her out made her feel faintly nauseous, as if she was being spied upon for unknown reasons. But that, of course, was ridiculous, she told herself firmly. Mrs Aspley and her former teachers had all agreed that she had far too much imagination for her own good.

The woman was old, desperate for

food or money and had perhaps overheard her telling the young mother where she lived. Or maybe it was all a coincidence. And she did still feel bad about dropping the shilling she was going to give this woman and letting a child steal it from under her nose. This was a way of salving her conscience.

She had barely had a chance to think this through to the end before she found herself in the hall, tugging open the heavy door, oblivious to the fact that, as far as the servants and her stepmother were concerned, she ought to have been upstairs, nursing her head.

At first she thought the old beggar-woman had gone. Then she caught sight of a hat with a broken and misshapen brim, a pair of stooping shoulders.

'Wait!'

Her cry came out louder than she intended, echoing against the buildings opposite. A flock of startled sparrows spluttered into the air. Diana ran down the steps towards the gate, leaving the door ajar behind her.

Fortunately the old woman had not gone far. She turned and started to shuffle back. Diana cast an agonised look towards the house. She wanted to meet the beggar-woman halfway, but was terrified Mrs Aspley might glance out of the window and see her.

'I'm so glad you came,' Diana exclaimed as soon as she judged the beggar-woman was within earshot. 'You *did* come to see me, didn't you? I'm so sorry about what happened yesterday.'

'Oh, bless your kind heart, miss, you've no cause to apologise to the likes of me,' the crone replied and once more Diana was taken aback by her expressionless face, so at odds with her words. 'In truth, I was in two minds if I should be bothering you at all.'

'No, no, you have every right to go wherever you choose,' Diana cut her short, 'Indeed, I am glad you're here. I felt so guilty about what happened and had no idea how I might find you again. I don't even know your name.'

The old woman gave her a twisted smile.

'Wouldn't do you much good if you did,' she replied. 'I daresay I'm not the only Mrs Jones in London, not by a long way.'

'No, I'm sure you're right.' Diana forced a smile to her lips, but still she couldn't suppress a tremor of unease, though she wasn't sure if it was the old woman that unnerved her so, or the possibility that her stepmother might catch her here. 'I can't stay long, but I hope you'll accept a small trifle for your trouble in coming all this way.'

Fortunately she had two shillings left in her purse amid the assortment of other coins. The old woman mumbled and demurred, but Diana dared not stay any longer. After a few last words, she flew back to the house and it only occurred to her as she leaned, panting, against the front door that she had been running again and that anyone might have seen it.

Moreover she could hear voices and

then the click of the drawing room door as it opened. There was no time to reach her bedroom or the back stairs. She had no option but to whip into the library again and hope against hope that Mrs Aspley wouldn't choose to investigate the opening and closing of various doors on the ground floor.

Her heart was still thumping, her breathing irregular. So much so, that she was surprised nobody could hear it, even through the thickness of the library door.

The footsteps and voices came closer. Evidently Mrs Aspley had decided that Mr Godolphin was too important a guest to be shown out of the house by a mere servant.

' . . . so grateful for all your help and advice.' Mrs Aspley's voice drifted down the stairs.

Mr Godolphin made some self-deprecating remark, but Mrs Aspley pressed on.

'You've been most understanding,' she said. 'And I know I can depend on your discretion on that other matter. Oh, I am sure Diana means well, but she is so unworldly that she is apt to make life very difficult for herself, and for others.'

Diana recoiled from the door. Could it be that Mr Godolphin had betrayed her trust by showing her stepmother the incriminating letter written in her own handwriting? She wanted to storm out of the library and confront him, but then she would have had to explain what she was doing there.

'I am willing to believe that her only fault is a little naïvety,' Mr Godolphin replied. 'Please tell Miss Aspley that I hope her headache will grow better soon.'

Mrs Aspley positively gushed at this, but Diana barely heard her. Her thoughts were whirling much too fast. Surely that reference to her supposed headache could only mean one thing — that Edgar Godolphin had not told her stepmother that he had talked to her that morning?

For the remainder of that morning, Diana was on tenterhooks. Despite what she had overheard, she kept expecting her stepmother to send for her and scold her for going against her wishes in the matter of Alice Simmonds.

But nothing happened. Mrs Aspley was cool when they did meet, it was true, but no more so than was usual after one of their disputes. Neither of them spoke much, both equally eager to avoid the possibility of a fresh quarrel, particularly as they were to attend a private ball that night.

Diana still did not know many people in London and she was not sure she was in the right frame of mind for dancing — until she entered the ballroom. Instantly she was dazzled by the flicker of a hundred candles, reflected in three long mirrors, which made it feel as if there were as many dancing flames as there were stars in the clear, country sky at home.

The excitement in the air was

palpable. Diana couldn't help being infected by it, despite her lurking fear that nobody would notice her and therefore nobody would ask her to dance.

She need not have worried. She had not been there ten minutes before her hostess introduced her to a fashionably dressed if callow-looking youth, who instantly asked her for the first two dances.

The ordeal was every bit as bad as she had feared. Her partner blundered through the dances, often setting off in the wrong direction when he forgot which figure came next. Diana felt as if the eyes of the whole of London were upon her. It was only when she was standing out at the top of the set that she realised most of the assembled company was too absorbed in conversation to be watching anyone, much less a nobody like herself.

She was surprised, therefore, that the second person to ask her to dance should be Edgar Godolphin. From the little she knew of him, he did not strike her as a man who danced much, and especially not the more boisterous country-dances that were currently in vogue.

But he acquitted himself much better than she had dared expect and it was not until they reached the foot of the longways set that she discovered he had an ulterior motive.

'I wanted an opportunity to speak to you,' he said, lowering his head so he could also lower his voice. 'It only occurred to me on my way home from your *step*mother's house that we have overlooked a few things in regard to your — quest.'

'Oh? How so?'

'Well, there are other ways to find a missing person besides advertising for information. It struck me that I might make enquiries in the neighbourhood in which you saw Miss Simmonds.'

'Oh.' Now he had said it, it seemed so logical. Indeed it had been the first idea that had occurred to her when she had been trying to decide how best to find Alice.

'Yes, of course. I never expected you to take so much trouble.'

Mr Godolphin waved this aside.

'The only difficulty I foresee is that I have never met Miss Simmonds and I don't think it will be possible for you to accompany me. I don't suppose you have a recent portrait of your friend?'

Diana's face brightened.

'Well, yes, in a manner of speaking. Not a professional portrait, but I do have some sketches in my portfolio from when we were at school together, though I'm afraid I was not the best artist in the class.'

'I hope there is at least a vague resemblance to the original,' Mr Godolphin replied dryly.

Diana found herself warming to Edgar Godolphin during the course of that dance and the one that followed it. Though he had struck her as aloof on first meeting him, she realised he had a quiet, understated sense of humour and she wondered if he deliberately chose not to compete with his mother's loquaciousness.

She was even half-sorry when the second dance was over, knowing that, according to etiquette, she would now be obliged to dance with someone else.

She had barely had a chance to sit down and cool her face with a flutter of her fan before she was approached by the hostess with an elegantly if under-statedly dressed gentleman in tow, whom Diana had noticed in the longways set.

'I trust you are enjoying yourself, Miss Aspley?' the matron asked.

'Very much so, thank you.'

'Good, good. May I present you to Mr Beaumont? Mr Beaumont, Miss Aspley of Nottingham.'

It did not occur to Diana to point out that it was possible to live in Notting-hamshire without actually living in Nottingham itself. The gentleman's name had caused a shiver to run down her spine. She had read and reread

Alice's letters so many times of late that she couldn't help wondering if this could be the same Mr Beaumont who had been invited to the Simmonds's house party on the Christmas before last.

They exchanged greetings and Diana was struck by the gentleness of Mr Beaumont's voice. When he led her towards the longways set, he held her hand so delicately, she could barely feel it at all.

'I admit I had an ulterior motive in asking to be introduced to you,' he said as they crossed the floor. He spoke so softly, she was obliged to tilt her head closer to catch his words above the general bustle in the ballroom.

'Indeed?' she replied, wondering if her name might have been familiar to him from Alice's stories.

'I could not help noticing that you were by far the most animated dancer in the set and I hoped I might be able to elicit the same beautiful smile as your previous partner.'

Diana could not help blushing and smiling behind her fan at such lavish compliments. It was not at all what she was used to.

'Ah, yes, there it is,' he cried out, making her blush even more.

'I fear, sir, I shall have to force myself to frown at you if you do not desist,' Diana replied, but her attempt to sound severe was undermined by the urge to giggle.

Mr Beaumont eyed her gravely as he replied. 'Ah, that would be a great pity. I suspect I should be much frightened by your frowns and would do my utmost to avoid them in the future, if you would only teach me the correct way of doing so.'

Diana was relieved that the obligation to dance saved her from having to find an answer, something that she felt was utterly beyond her at present. She found she could not make up her mind about her partner. If he was indeed the same Mr Beaumont that Alice had mentioned in her letters, she understood exactly why her friend had been charmed by him.

But could a man who had professed to be Alice's admirer flirt so easily with a stranger? It was true that a year had passed since Alice's fall from grace, but could a devoted heart recover so quickly after being wounded?

But there Diana checked herself. Alice had never told her that any of her admirers had made any professions of love. Maybe she had made too much of what her friend had told her in her letters.

Determinedly she set her brooding aside and launched herself into the dance instead. It was one of the longer, more complicated dances and therefore required some concentration, but once they had progressed several places down the set, she began to feel more at ease.

She could not help but notice the hard look that one particular gentleman gave first her, then her partner. Mr

Beaumont, too, seemed to flinch when he caught sight of the other man, before he drew himself up straight.

The stranger was a tall, thin man, with dark hair and a hooked nose, not handsome by any stretch of the imagination, but so distinguished-looking that Diana felt instantly awed by him. When the dance obliged her to turn with her corner, he gripped her hands so hard that it made her glance up at his face in astonishment.

This appeared to be exactly what the stranger had wanted, because he leaned his head closer to hers and whispered one word.

'Beware.'

An Unpleasant Situation

Diana was so shocked by the implied threat, she came to an abrupt standstill. It was only because her partner whispered reminders and physically guided her into the right positions that she managed to stumble through the rest of the dance.

It had not escaped her attention that Mr Beaumont had cast a reproachful glare at the dark stranger, but the latter did not seem the least perturbed. Hostility bristled between the men. Diana felt as if she had blundered into a nightmare, which was made all the more sinister by the glittering atmosphere of the ballroom and her own previous light-heartedness.

She still felt shaken by the time she and Mr Beaumont had danced all the way to the foot of the set where they could momentarily catch their breath.

'You seem distressed, Miss Aspley,' Mr Beaumont murmured.

'I — well — who was that man?'

Mr Beaumont did not seem to need to be informed whom she meant.

'His name is Drake. A man of no family, or so I believe, and a scoundrel if there ever was one.'

The conjunction of the names was the last proof Diana needed.

'Oh, then you must be the same Mr Beaumont who stayed with the Simmonds last Christmas,' she exclaimed, causing her partner to jump, though she barely noticed. Her mind was too intent on its own calculations as she turned towards the other dancers and tried to pick out Mr Drake amid the seething mass.

'And that man I suppose must be . . . ' Her words trailed away, discretion belatedly catching up with the rapidity of her tongue.

She sensed rather than saw that Mr Beaumont had grown rigid at her words and when she glanced up, she was alarmed by the stricken look on his face.

'The Simmonds?' he echoed hollowly. 'Do you mean the George Simmonds of Leicestershire?'

Diana's face brightened, but her smile wavered when he did not respond to it.

'Yes,' she said. 'Alice Simmonds and I were at school together. I was supposed to go and stay with her that Christmas, but then Papa died and I couldn't go . . . '

She was talking far too fast, simply to fill in the silence. For some reason, Mr Beaumont would not meet her eye. Perhaps he did not know that she knew what had happened to Alice, or maybe there was another reason why any reference, however vague, to that time brought back painful memories.

'May I offer you a word of advice, Miss Aspley?' The words were spoken so softly, she could barely hear them above the music.

'Certainly, sir.'

'Stay as far away from John Drake as you can.'

Diana glanced up at her partner's face for confirmation that she had understood him correctly. But there was no time left. All along the longways set, couples cast down or led up to change places and it was time to launch themselves back into the fray.

It troubled Diana, as they worked their way towards the opposite end of the set, that she would be obliged to dance with John Drake again. She could not avoid holding hands with him, even if she shrank from his touch. She could not avoid being close enough for him to speak to her again. All she could do was lift her chin and stare through him, as if he was not even there, to show him how much she despised the man, who, she was almost convinced, must be Alice's seducer and the father of her baby.

She was quite proud of the way she acquitted herself. She thought she perceived Mr Drake frown at her uncharacteristically haughty air and it gave her courage to persist in the same course of action whenever she was obliged to dance with him. Mr Beaumont made no further comment, but Diana could sense his approval in the warmth of his smile.

Instead when they had an opportunity to speak, he asked her about her family and how she was enjoying London. When he discovered this was her first Season, he asked what she had seen already and suggested other places of interest.

Much though she loved dancing, Diana decided that if she was obliged to sit out the next two dances for lack of a partner, she would not have minded in the slightest if it meant conversing a little longer with Mr Beaumont.

She caught Mr Drake watching her from across the ballroom as her partner escorted her back to her seat, but fortunately the former gentleman seemed deeply immersed in conversation when Diana began to cough because her throat was so dry from her exertions. Mr Beaumont was all solicitude.

'I shall be back in a moment with a glass of wine,' he promised.

But she had not been seated for more than a minute when a shadow interposed itself between her and the light. She glanced up, intending to smile at the newcomer. Instead her breath caught in a gasp and she sprang to her feet.

'Please, do not be alarmed, Miss Aspley,' Mr Drake said. 'I know we have not been formally introduced, but I believe you are under a misapprehension about my character . . . '

'Oh no, I don't believe I am,' Diana replied, drawing herself up to her full height so she would not be so intimidated by his height. 'I think I know rather more about you than you believe I do.'

She knew she was overstating the case. But why else would Mr Beaumont warn her against this man if he were not a practised rake?

'Am I to take it then that Mr Beaumont is an old and trusted friend?' he asked.

Diana could not help blushing. She was too honest to lie about her acquaintance with Mr Beaumont, but nor was she willing to concede the point so easily.

'No, but I believe we have another mutual acquaintance,' she replied, tilting her chin in defiance.

It was an impulsive risk. Diana knew that bandying Alice's name about in public was not the most prudent thing to do, if Drake demanded to know to whom she was referring.

'Indeed? And who might that be?' Mr Drake raised his eyebrows.

'Oh, an impeccable source. I trust her judgement implicitly.'

Except, of course, it was Alice's lack of judgement that had presumably led to her downfall. But Diana was determined to bluff her way through the conversation as best she could until

Mr Beaumont returned. She glanced round to see if she could spot him. Instead she caught the eye of Mr Godolphin over the head of the lady with whom he was conversing.

'I take it, then, that I am not to be informed of the name of my defamer.'

The amusement in Mr Drake's voice made Diana flush. He was not taking her seriously.

'No, it is wrong of me to tease you,' Mr Drake went on before Diana could gather her wits. 'I apologise wholeheartedly. But you know not what grave peril you stand in by being too open and too trusting of strangers.'

Diana parted her lips, but more in astonishment than because she could find the right words to say. Mr Drake's words were such an uncanny echo of things her stepmother had said to her in the past that she almost suspected him of spying on her.

'A clever device, Drake, to warn a young lady against yourself,' Mr Beaumont's voice intervened so suddenly that Diana jumped. 'Then she will have nobody to blame but herself if her fingers get burnt.'

An angry flush appeared in Mr Drake's cheeks.

'I pray you, do not judge others by yourself,' he replied in biting tones. 'I do not believe there are many men who could match your standard of hypocrisy.'

Instead of reddening, Mr Beaumont grew deadly pale.

'I would advise you to keep a civil tongue in your head, if you do not wish me to call you out,' he said, his voice dropping to an even softer, more insidious tone.

His words sent a chill to Diana's heart.

'If you think I am afraid of you, you are very much mistaken,' Mr Drake retorted.

'Oh, please, stop it. There's no need for any of this,' Diana could not help intervening.

Her thoughts were galloping. The

gentlemen had kept their voices low enough not to attract public attention yet, but there would be no hiding the scandal of a duel. Diana's name would inevitably be linked with the affair, even though the real cause was obviously an old animosity between the two men.

Mr Beaumont bowed towards her.

'I would not dream of doing anything that would distress you, madam,' he said.

'A pretty way for you to conceal your cowardice,' Mr Drake murmured, smiling so patronisingly that Diana was convinced the other man would not be able to resist the provocation.

She uttered a cry of dismay.

'Miss Aspley?'

Yet another voice made Diana whirl round to face Edgar Godolphin.

'I believe you promised me these two dances, did you not?' he went on. 'If you will excuse us, gentlemen.' And before she knew what was happening Mr Godolphin had taken her hand and started leading her towards the centre of the room.

'Oh, but ... ' she stammered, glancing over her shoulder one more time at the adversaries.

'Hush, child,' her partner murmured. 'I apologise for taking this liberty, but I thought it better to rescue you from what looked like a perilous situation. I gather that those two gentlemen have been at daggers drawn for quite some time and I would not wish you to be innocently dragged into their disputes.'

'Oh.' Diana was not sure what to make of this. 'I — I suppose I ought to thank you.'

But she glanced back one more time, half-afraid that she would see some indication that the dispute had resumed or, worse still, that Messrs Beaumont and Drake had decided to dispense with formalities and had engaged in some manner of duel on the spot.

But Mr Beaumont had apparently withdrawn from the room, while Mr Drake was still glowering at her from beneath lowered eyebrows.

'And now, Miss Aspley,' Mr Godolphin said in a brisk tone, 'I hope you will deign to glance at me now and then and perhaps smile occasionally so that you don't start a rumour that we have quarrelled bitterly or that I have done you some irreparable injury.'

Diana tried to resist, but a smile spread across her face despite her best efforts.

'That's much better,' Mr Godolphin pronounced, just as the music began.

Those two dances proved to be the last before the set broke up at suppertime. Mrs Aspley seemed in excellent spirits when she rejoined Diana at the supper table and she even complimented her stepdaughter on how pretty she was looking. Even so, Diana found herself brooding on the disagreement between Mr Beaumont and Mr Drake.

It was only after supper, when partners were being chosen and sets formed for the quadrilles that something happened to change the direction of Diana's thoughts.

'I declare, Mr Godolphin, you have surprised me tonight.'

At the sound of the familiar name, Diana could not help glancing round. Mr Godolphin was not far from her, but his back was turned towards her.

'How so?'

'Well.' The stately blonde beauty who had accosted him simpered behind her fan. 'I don't believe I have ever seen you dance twice with the same partner in a single evening in all the time I have known you.'

'The child is new in town and hardly knows a soul,' Mr Godolphin replied indifferently. 'And you must have noticed how much she relishes dancing. It would be a shame to see her sitting out.'

Diana swallowed her indignation with difficulty. Mrs Aspley had often warned her that she would be regarded as a hoyden if she did not learn to be more sedate. But *the child*! Could he not have found some other epithet by which to refer to her?

'You never used to be so philan-thropic,' the stately beauty replied, shaking her head. 'You had better keep your wits about you. You would not wish to be caught in a trap, would you? And if you dance so much with one lady this week and far less with another next week, comparisons will be made and conclusions drawn.'

Diana saw Mr Godolphin's shoulders stiffen and she suspected he was frowning.

All he said, however, was, 'Tongues will wag amongst idle people, whether there is anything worth discussing or not.'

★   ★   ★

As convention demanded, Edgar God-olphin called on the Aspleys the following morning, nominally to enquire after his dancing partner's health. And naturally Mrs Aspley made no difficulties when, after a discussion about the ball, Mr

Godolphin expressed an interest in seeing Diana's portfolio.

She complied somewhat grudgingly. She knew why it was important, but the remarks she had overheard the previous evening still rankled. Mrs Aspley made a point of keeping at bay the callow youth with whom Diana had danced first, by engaging him in a conversation about his parentage and prospects, no matter how much the boy squirmed and cast longing looks at the pair at the opposite end of the spacious room.

With the memory of the oil paintings at the Foundling Hospital still fresh in her mind, Diana found herself blushing more than usual at her sketches and watercolours, but Mr Godolphin was scrupulously polite in his comments as they turned the pages.

Diana felt acutely conscious of his proximity, his shoulder sometimes brushing against hers as he leaned closer, or his fingers accidentally touching hers as they both reached for the same page.

Diana had taken care to rearrange

her portfolio so the sketches of Alice would be near the beginning, but sufficiently hidden amid her watercolours so her stepmother would not find them too soon if she had picked up the portfolio for one reason or another.

'This is the picture I particularly wanted you to see,' Diana said, casting a surreptitious look at her stepmother. 'I think it's my best attempt at the subject.'

For a long time Mr Godolphin said nothing, his eyes fixed on the sketch of the pretty, fair-haired girl. Diana ventured a quick glance up at him. It was not often that she was able to gaze so closely at such a handsome man. She noticed the sweep of his lashes on his half-lowered eyelids, the curl of his ear, the way the light fell, emphasising his cheekbone and bringing out the dapple of stubble along his cleanly-shaven jaw.

Without moving his head, Mr Godolphin raised his eyes and caught her watching him. Diana flushed as she dropped her gaze.

'Gracious, Miss Aspley, anyone would think you had decided to try your hand at painting my portrait,' he drawled, making her blush even more fiercely.

'Oh no, I'm sure I am not talented enough to do justice to the subject,' she murmured.

Mr Godolphin uttered a brief laugh, scarcely more than an expulsion of breath.

'Is that a compliment?' he asked.

'If you like.'

But Diana was disconcerted when she glanced up and found her step-mother watching her with something that looked uncannily like approval.

She thinks I'm trying to ensnare him. Whereas Diana was not at all sure she was capable of ensnaring any man, let alone this one.

It was a relief when Mr Beaumont was announced, even though Mr Godolphin eyed him somewhat warily. Fortunately both gentlemen were far too discreet to make any reference to the unpleasantness the previous evening, though Mr Beaumont apologised profusely when he managed to snatch a moment alone with Diana and assured her there was no danger of a duel.

His charming manners swiftly won over Mrs Aspley, who had only met him briefly at the ball. Diana could not help noticing that by contrast Mr Godolphin did not show himself to his best advantage, as he grew more withdrawn with every minute that passed.

Having complimented both ladies on their looks and the charming arrangement of the furniture in the room, Mr Beaumont's eye fell upon a side table.

'And is this your portfolio, Miss Aspley?' he asked, turning doe eyes upon her. 'Do let me see.'

Even if she had wanted to refuse, Diana could not think of a single excuse, particularly as she had already granted the privilege to Mr Godolphin. She knew Mr Beaumont was overly indulgent about her efforts, but he did it in such an unostentatious fashion that she could not help but smile and shake her head at him.

And then he turned the page and his expression changed. Diana hardly dared breathe. She did not need to look down to deduce that he had stumbled upon the portraits of Alice Simmonds.

After what felt like an age, he uttered a profound sigh and stroked the page as reverently as if it had been a religious relic.

'Ah, I would not have thought it possible for someone who is not a professional portraitist to have caught such a look of sweetness and innocence,' he murmured.

'You flatter me, sir.' Diana fanned herself to try to cool her scarlet cheeks.

'Oh no, indeed, I never flatter,' Mr Beaumont assured her, gazing so deeply into her eyes that she felt dizzy.

'Miss Aspley, will you be at the theatre tomorrow night?'

The abruptness of Mr Godolphin's question made Diana jump.

'Oh yes, indeed,' Mrs Aspley intervened hastily. 'Your mother was kind enough to invite us both to join her in her box. I trust that you will also be there?'

Mr Godolphin bowed his assent. But Mrs Aspley had not done with him yet. She positively fawned upon him and made sure he knew of every invitation she had accepted for the coming week, in the hopes that they might meet at the townhouses of mutual acquaintances or in some place of public entertainment.

Diana could sense Mr Godolphin stiffening again, his answers growing briefer by the minute. Mr Beaumont did his best to distract Diana, but she could not help being disturbed by Mrs Aspley's blatant matchmaking. The thought that Mr Godolphin might think she was throwing herself at him was intolerable.

So, while Mrs Aspley was saying farewell to their other callers, Diana snatched the opportunity to murmur, 'I really am sorry about my stepmother. She really is desperate to marry me off and . . . '

She drew herself up short and bit her lip. This was just the kind of impetuousness she was always being scolded about.

But to her surprise and relief, Mr Godolphin's face relaxed and he laughed.

'Really, Miss Aspley,' he said in conscious imitation of her, 'I don't think I have ever met a young lady quite like you.'

There was no time for any more conversation, but after he had gone, Diana was left pondering over whether those words were meant as a criticism or a compliment.

'Well, Diana, you seem to have made a conquest,' her stepmother remarked once the door had closed behind their visitors.

'Mr Beaumont, you mean?' Diana asked. 'Oh no, I have it on good authority that he . . . '

But she did not have a chance to finish her denial.

'No, no, don't pretend you did not

notice how jealous Mr Godolphin became when you paid so much attention to Mr Beaumont.'

'Jealous? Mr Godolphin?' Diana stared at her blankly, not sure whether her stepmother had not finally taken leave of her senses.

'Of course. Why else would he be so eager to break up your little tête-à-tête and discover how you intend to spend the next days?'

Diana forbore to point out that Mrs Aspley had volunteered far more than she had been asked.

'No, that can't be right. Mr Godolphin doesn't even *like* me very much. He thinks I'm a child.'

But Mrs Aspley shook her head with a self-satisfied smile that Diana suspected nothing would shift.

'Oh Diana, you have so very much to learn about the ways of gentlemen,' she said. 'Why do you suppose he was so determined to outstay Mr Beaumont, or to have a private word with you before he left?'

And since Diana could not explain to her stepmother what their last exchange had really been about, she was forced to be silent.

The First Replies

Diana's limited fund of patience was tested to its utmost over the course of the following week. The advertisement did not appear in the newspaper as quickly as she had hoped. She even began to suspect Mr Godolphin had never sent it and that she would have to write it for a third time and then confront the perfidious traitor who thought he could hoodwink her as if she was a child.

Even after the advertisement had finally been published, things didn't grow any easier. She found herself brooding on it constantly, wondering if any replies had arrived yet and whether she could trust Mr Godolphin to pass all the letters on to her.

To add to her disappointment, she had seen nothing more of Mr Beaumont in all that time. It would have been a pleasure to be able to talk to somebody who knew Alice.

Diana was also more than a little sorry she had not told him that she had seen her friend. An additional pair of eyes would have been useful in their quest. She was sure Mr Beaumont must be liberal-minded enough to forgive Alice's lapse. She had considered broaching the matter with Mr Godolphin, but she felt awkward about having to explain why she had not mentioned Mr Beaumont's connection with Alice sooner.

To compensate for this omission, wherever she went, Diana found herself gazing out of the carriage window, scanning faces, searching for Alice. But she knew that, even in the safety of a carriage, she would never be allowed to venture into the worst slums, where a fugitive was most likely to be hiding.

All in all, she was beginning to lose hope that she would be able to do anything useful until one day Mrs Godolphin arrived on a morning call, accompanied by her son. They were not the first guests to be shown into the drawing room and as a result, there was absolutely no chance of any private conversation.

Diana was therefore taken aback when Edgar Godolphin addressed her.

'By the way, Miss Aspley, I brought you that book I was telling you about the other day,' he said, fishing in the pocket of his coat.

'Book?' Diana looked blank.

'Yes, you remember the one. I thought perhaps you might peruse it and then tell me what you think.' His eyes remained fixed upon hers and belatedly Diana realised what he was hinting at.

'Oh. Oh, yes, of course, I'd quite forgotten,' she said, taking the book with trembling hands. 'Thank you very much.'

He inclined his head.

'My pleasure.'

'Well, Mr Godolphin,' Mrs Aspley intervened. 'You must have worked miracles on the girl. She was never much of a one for books in the past, or so her schoolteachers informed her father. Much too restless and talkative.'

'That's not quite true,' Diana objected. 'I've always had a passion for novels.'

Mrs Aspley sniffed meaningfully.

'No wonder your head is so full of nonsense and strange fancies,' she said and then, belatedly recalling that she ought to be showing off her stepdaughter's better qualities rather than her faults, she hastily changed tack. 'Still, I suppose it is not possible to have an old, wise head on young shoulders. I hope by and by we may find the right man to guide and form your mind so that you will become the first ornament of society.'

Diana did not reply in words, but she averted her face so she could roll her eyes expressively. Any man who attempted to form her mind would find that it was no easy task he had undertaken.

To Diana, the visiting hour seemed to

last for an eternity. Even after the first guests had departed to pay their next call, new visitors arrived to take their place.

In parting Mr Godolphin managed to murmur, 'Remember, do nothing until you have talked to me,' but there was no time for her to respond.

His words made her more excited than ever, convincing her there must be something of importance in the letters. So it came as a surprise, when she had finally conveyed the book to the peace of her bedchamber to discover all three letters hidden between the pages were still sealed and unread.

Diana felt strangely touched that Edgar Godolphin apparently respected her judgement enough to allow her to read the letters on her own — and that he trusted her to show them to him afterwards.

Hardly daring to breathe, she broke the seal of the first letter. It was an ill-spelt scrawl by someone who evidently did not handle a pen very often, informing her that a young lady matching Alice's description lodged in the next room to the informant.

Diana felt relief flood through her. Perhaps it would be a simpler process than she had dared hope to find Alice, though the question of how to help her friend once she had been found still had not been settled. She hardly thought the other letters were worth opening, but she did so since someone had evidently taken the trouble to write to her.

It was just as well she did. The letters gave completely different information, suggesting different parts of London in which she ought to conduct her search. And when she examined the letters side by side, it dawned on her that the information in all three was exceedingly vague and that there were hints that, since the lady might not be easy to persuade to return to her friends, some of the reward might be given in advance to the informant, as proof of goodwill or to cover the expenses those infor- mants had incurred while searching for the missing lady or helping her when she was in dire need.

The more she reread the letters, the less Diana knew whom to believe. Was Alice living in a garret in Spitalfields, or working as a seamstress at the poorer end of Soho?

Much though it hurt her pride to admit it, she would need Edgar Godolphin's help to find Alice, as he had known from the start.

* * *

'Well?' Edgar Godolphin asked. There was no need for him to say any more. Diana knew from his tone exactly what he meant.

She had been on tenterhooks all day and her stepmother had accused her of growing more flighty than ever when she had misheard a question and answered something entirely beside the point.

Diana had been counting the hours till evening, desperately hoping that Mr Godolphin would be at the opera too, but fearing that even if he was, they would not have an opportunity to speak.

But with some assistance from Mrs Aspley, Mr Godolphin had contrived to obtain a seat just behind Diana.

'I don't know,' Diana admitted. 'They all say something different.'

Even without looking round, she could sense Mr Godolphin's face had relaxed into a rueful smile. It was as well that the fashionable world came to the Opera House not to listen but to gossip and to be seen in their finery. Under the double cover of the music and the murmur of voices around them, it was easier for them to talk than she had dared hope.

'I did warn you it would not be easy,' he said. 'There are plenty of unscrupulous and desperate people in this city.'

Diana sighed. She felt dispirited for once. If she could have been doing something active, it would not have been so terrible. But to be confined as she was by propriety and her stepmother's watchful eye . . .

'Fortunately we are not entirely dependent on replies to the newspaper article,' Mr Godolphin said, still in the same undertone.

Diana's eyes had been fixed on the stage, but now she could not help glancing back at him.

'Oh, have you discovered something?'

Mr Godolphin threw a look one way, then the other.

'Not here,' he said, lowering his voice till it was scarce above a breath. 'But perhaps if the weather holds fair tomorrow, I could take you for a drive in Hyde Park?'

Diana flushed in spite of herself and fluttered her fan in a vain attempt to cool her face.

★   ★   ★

Diana knew her restlessness the following morning was annoying her stepmother, but she could not seem to settle. Every ten minutes or so, she found herself wandering across to the drawing room window, in an agony lest the clouds should gather and a sudden shower put paid to her planned tête-à-tête with Edgar Godolphin.

It had been agreed between Diana and Mr Godolphin that their meeting in Hyde Park should be contrived to look like an accident. She had had some doubts about her ability to persuade her stepmother to go for a drive in the park at the fashionable hour, but she had underestimated Mrs Aspley's desire to be seen in all the right places.

Indeed she even seemed pleased that her stepdaughter was finally taking some of her advice seriously. Diana could not help feeling a trifle uneasy at the unmerited praise as she took her seat beside her stepmother.

It was some time before they chanced upon Mr Godolphin. The park was crowded because of the fine weather and more than once Mrs Aspley ordered the carriage to stop so she could gossip with an acquaintance. Diana was growing restless again when at last they were accosted by a familiar voice.

'Oh, Mrs Aspley, Miss Aspley, how delightful to see you both.'

Just the sound of Mrs Godolphin's voice made Diana's face light up.

'My dears, you will never believe who I just saw, promenading in her chariot as if she were the Queen of England,' Mrs Godolphin was already rattling away.

Diana exchanged glances with Edgar Godolphin. He was sitting beside his mother, the reins of his curricle resting loosely in his hands, a secretive smile upon his lips. Perhaps he saw the fever of impatience Diana was in, because he only waited until his mother stopped to draw breath before he intervened.

'I'm sure you and Mrs Aspley must have a great deal to talk about, Mamma,' he said. 'What would you say if I took Miss Aspley for a little turn and allowed you to speak more comfortably?'

Mrs Aspley looked pleased rather than disapproving at the suggestion. It took only a matter of minutes for Diana to exchange seats with Mrs Godolphin and it was only as Mr Godolphin took her hand to assist her into the curricle that Diana felt a flutter of unease at being so completely alone with a man she barely knew, even in the midst of an ogling crowd.

But this was for Alice's sake, Diana reminded herself firmly.

'I believe you have some news for me?' she asked as soon as the curricle was out of earshot of her stepmother's carriage.

'You don't waste any time on idle chatter, I see,' he replied, but then took pity on her. 'Yes, well, I'm not sure I have found Miss Simmonds as yet, but I've found trace of a young mother and supposed widow matching her description, who is eking out a living by taking in casual sewing. She has been seen in the vicinity in which you saw your friend, though the people I have spoken to seem not to know exactly where she lives, or so they claim. It's all very tenuous, I'm afraid, but . . . '

'No, that sounds extremely promising,' Diana cut his apologies short. 'I can't thank you enough for all the time and trouble you have taken.'

Mr Godolphin smiled wryly.

'But my question remains the same — what are you going to do with Miss Simmonds and her child if — when we find her?'

For a second she toyed with the idea of telling him what she had in mind.

'Oh, I don't know. Perhaps she or I could write to her parents and try to forge a reconciliation that way?' Diana suggested.

Mr Godolphin looked grim, however.

'I would not raise your hopes too high on that score,' he said. 'I've made a few casual enquiries among my acquaintances and from what I can make out, Miss Simmonds was already expecting her child before she came to London. There were some whispers about how plump she was growing during her time here and the rumour is that when her father realised what a fool she had made of him, as he saw it, he cast her out of the house with only the clothes she stood up in.

'Certainly you were not the only person to have been informed that she is dead. That is in fact the generally accepted story and it will only add to the difficulty in resurrecting her, as it were, if we can rescue her from whatever her current mode of life might be.'

Diana felt shocked, in spite of herself, and she could not help feeling relieved that she had seen Alice before she heard this rumour. But still a little nagging voice at the back of her head troubled her. Suppose it wasn't Alice I saw. Suppose she really is dead . . .

The thought was too horrible to contemplate.

It felt like an omen that the sun burst out from behind a fair-weather cloud at that very moment. Diana's face brightened too.

'I might speak to my mother about providing shelter for Miss Simmonds, though I would rather not say anything to her until we have found our fugitive.' Mr Godolphin looked apologetic. 'I love my mother very much, but sometimes she is not entirely discreet and I feel it would be better for this matter to remain secret until we have some positive results.'

'Oh, you really are wonderful. I could not ask for a better ally.' The words escaped Diana before she could stop them and she reddened as Mr Godolphin gave her a quizzical look. Then, unable to resist a moment longer, he burst into laughter.

'Really, Miss Aspley, I am flattered by your good opinion,' he said, shaking his head and still laughing, 'but I am not sure you should allow your stepmother — or indeed any other lady of a similar age and temperament — hear you express yourself with quite so much enthusiasm.'

Diana's blush deepened, but she

couldn't help smiling too as she averted her face.

'Well,' Mr Godolphin said in a brisker tone. 'You had better tell me all about the replies you have had to the advertisement.'

Diana told him what she knew as succinctly as she could. His eyes remained fixed on his horses' ears and a slight frown creased his forehead.

'I wonder,' he said. 'Would you trust me with the letters?'

'Yes, I suppose so,' Diana agreed, but still she frowned. 'They're in a hidden compartment in my desk at home.'

'Ah, well, then I shall be forced to call upon you and your stepmother tomorrow morning,' Mr Godolphin replied. 'Perhaps you can slip them into my book and return them that way. Unless you too are going to be at the Watsons' crush tonight?'

'My stepmother insists upon it,' Diana replied with a rueful smile.

⋆   ⋆   ⋆

Diana was still brooding about all she had learnt as they trundled back towards the townhouse. She barely noticed that her stepmother had been talking ceaselessly, repeating gossip she had learnt from Mrs Godolphin.

And then her ear was caught by an all too familiar name.

'It's a miracle Mr Beaumont wasn't killed,' Mrs Aspley said, shaking her head.

'Killed?' Diana echoed, a chill creeping across her skin like an army of spiders. 'What happened?'

'He was injured in a duel over the honour of some silly girl who allowed herself to be seduced.'

Diana groaned and closed her eyes, remembering the scene in the ballroom. And it wasn't for some minutes that Diana realised belatedly that her stepmother had no idea who the woman at the centre of this scandal was.

The Search Begins

'Have you heard?' Diana was in much too much of a ferment to observe social niceties and blurted out the question as soon as she found herself alone with Mr Godolphin.

It had struck her as soon as she entered the Watsons's drawing room that the word 'crush' was entirely apt for this gathering. There were more people here than the room could comfortably hold and it had been no easy matter for Diana to catch sight of Mr Godolphin, let alone get close him.

'Heard what?' Mr Godolphin raised an eyebrow at her.

'That Mr Beaumont and Mr Drake have had a duel about Alice.'

Mr Godolphin had looked quizzical as she rattled on, but at her last two words, his frown deepened.

'About Alice?' he repeated. 'What

makes you think the duel was about her?'

'Oh, it must have been about her,' Diana insisted. 'My stepmother told me that Mr Beaumont had accused Mr Drake of seducing an innocent girl and they fought and now Mr Beaumont is at death's door and who knows where Mr Drake might be lurking . . . '

Her breath caught in her throat, blocking off the other words that churned inside her.

'Firstly, let me put your mind at ease. Far from being at death's door, Mr Beaumont escaped with a mere scratch. To my knowledge he has already received close friends and well-wishers. It's true the initial report of his condition was much more grave, which is why Mr Drake has gone abroad for his own safety,' Mr Godolphin said.

'But as for the cause of the duel, you seem to have got the details backwards,' Mr Godolphin went on. 'It was Mr Drake who accused Mr Beaumont of seducing a lady, whose name he refused to divulge, though Beaumont seemed to know well enough to whom he was referring.'

For a moment, Diana was thunderstruck, her mind twisting and whirling, trying to make sense of what she had just heard.

'Oh, the devious villain,' she breathed. 'To have twisted things around and accused another man of his own crime, and then hurt *him* in a duel that he himself had instigated, almost forced the other man to demand . . . '

'You are determined, then, to see poor Drake in the blackest possible light?'

Diana couldn't conceal her astonishment.

'What other way is there to see this case?' she asked. 'It's as clear as day who the villain is.' She groped frantically for some irrefutable evidence. 'Mr Beaumont warned me that Mr Drake was a scoundrel. And then there are Alice's letters.'

'You have letters?' Mr Godolphin

interrupted her. 'Directly accusing her seducer?'

Diana flushed.

'N-no, not exactly,' she admitted reluctantly. 'But now that I know, it's all so obvious. Oh, I'm not explaining this the right way. I was meant to spend that Christmas with Alice and her family, but I couldn't go because Papa died, so I asked her to write and tell me all about it and she did. Mr Drake and Mr Beaumont were both staying with the Simmonds that Christmas, so you see I know all about their characters from Alice's descriptions.'

'Pardon me, but I am afraid I do not share your faith in Miss Simmonds's ability to judge characters correctly.'

The words were spoken quietly, but they felt like a slap to the face.

'Forgive me,' Edgar Godolphin said in a low tone. 'I did not mean to upset you by casting aspersions on your friend when the truth is she is more likely to have been deceived by a consummate actor than by someone who is obviously a rake.'

Diana blinked and cleared her throat.

'That is very — noble of you,' she managed to croak.

★ ★ ★

It was, by Diana's calculation, the sixth draper's shop they had stopped at in as many minutes, in order to examine the wares in the window. She suppressed a sigh. She had no doubt it was very prudent of her stepmother to choose the best quality damask she could afford for the new tablecloths.

But all the same, Diana was grateful that Mrs Godolphin had joined them on this shopping expedition and could discuss the merits of each potential purchase with Mrs Aspley because, left to her own devices, Diana would have long since run out of things to say.

Three days had passed since her last private conversation with Edgar Godolphin and once again her patience had been tried to its utmost. She half-regretted returning the letters to Mr Godolphin, or at least not keeping copies. Her mind had been perpetually churning, trying to recall every precise detail in case she had missed something.

Her eye snagged upon a familiar figure, though it took her a moment to recall where she had seen the woman before.

It seemed like an omen. Diana cast a hasty glance at her companions, to ascertain that neither of them would notice if she slipped away. And then she was hurrying towards the baker's shop, where two small urchins, aged no more than three or four, were standing on tiptoe in order to press their noses against the glass and eye the fragrant, newly baked bread they would never be able to afford.

'Mrs Jones,' Diana called, pleased she had remembered the name.

The shabbily dressed woman, standing behind the urchins and carrying a still younger child straddled across her hip, turned her head sharply at the sound of her name, her eyes narrowing.

'You remember me, don't you?' Diana's voice faltered, but she forced herself to go on. 'We met a few weeks ago, when I got lost, and then you came to my stepmother's townhouse in Portman Square . . . '

'I remember.'

The laconic response was not quite what Diana had anticipated.

'Are these the grandchildren you told me about?' Diana persisted. 'Poor little mites. I'm an orphan too, you know. Perhaps you'd accept a small trifle so you could buy them some bread or something?'

The words were rattling out so quickly now that Diana herself could hardly keep up with them. Nerves always made her more loquacious than perhaps was wise and besides, she knew she had little time before one of her chaperones would notice her absence.

'Very generous of you, ma'am,' Mrs

Jones replied, shifting the infant to settle it more comfortably on her hip. 'Now if there was ever anything I could do for you . . . '

'Oh, but there is,' Diana interjected, ignoring the odd sensation in her stomach which hinted that perhaps Mrs Jones had not meant the words literally. 'That is to say — you remember the day when we first met?'

Mrs Jones nodded warily, hastily pocketing the shilling Diana had offered her.

'Well, the reason I was lost was because — well, I'd spied an old friend of mine who has come down in the world and I ran after her, but she disappeared and I think it might be possible she lives somewhere in that part of London, only I can't look for her myself. So I thought you might be able to help me find her,' Diana stumbled on. 'Her name is Alice Simmonds, but I suppose she might have changed it. She has fair hair and blue eyes and when I saw her that day, she was wearing a bottle green pelisse and she has a baby, a little younger than your youngest grandchild . . . '

She faltered, remembering Mr Godolphin's strictures about not revealing the existence of Alice's baby to all and sundry. But she had not known how else she might describe Alice to Mrs Jones in a way she would recognise.

'Oh, is that the way it is?' the older woman replied at last, her mouth pursing. 'You know it'll not be an easy task or a quick one. Plenty of young girls that, well . . . ' She shrugged, biting off whatever cant phrase had been on her lips.

'Yes, I know and I'll pay you for your time and trouble. But you will look and ask around, won't you?'

Diana cast a glance over her shoulder, to check if her stepmother was still preoccupied, and so she missed Mrs Jones's reaction.

'I'll try,' the older woman said grudgingly. 'Can't promise you I'll be successful.'

'Oh, thank you. You've no idea how grateful I am . . . '

'Diana!'

She let go of Mrs Jones's fingers, which she had squeezed in her enthusiasm.

'Here.' She found another sixpence in her purse and pressed it into the older woman's hand. 'If you come back to the house, I'll tell the cook to give you whatever she can spare from the kitchen.'

*   *   *

Diana spent a sleepless night, wondering if she ought to confess what she had done to Mr Godolphin. On the one hand, she hoped that her efforts might eventually yield good results. But on the other hand, she feared that he might disagree and, worse still, that he might be proved correct.

She was still undecided how best to proceed when she next had an opportunity to speak to Mr Godolphin in private. They were strolling through St James's Park, with her stepmother trailing at a discreet distance behind them with a friend.

'So,' Diana asked, as soon as was consistent with politeness, 'how is the quest proceeding?'

Mr Godolphin smiled wryly.

'That depends upon your point of view,' he replied. 'The Spitalfields letter is a mere attempt to extort money and it looks as if the Seven Dials letter will prove similarly unsatisfactory.'

'Oh.' Diana felt herself deflate.

'But from another perspective, it's as well to dismiss false trails as soon as possible in order to follow more promising ones.'

'Yes, I suppose so,' Diana replied.

'And wouldn't you rather your friend was in Soho than in Seven Dials?' Mr Godolphin persisted.

Diana mustered a smile.

'Yes. Yes, of course. If it *is* her.'

'If it is her,' he concurred. He glanced over his shoulder to make sure nobody was within earshot. 'Do you have something to write upon? I have the address of the mantua-maker in Soho who may employ your friend and I thought it would be more easy for you to call there and see for yourself whether or not any of the seamstresses is Miss Simmonds.'

'Truly?' Diana's face brightened. 'You really think you have found her?'

He shrugged. 'Possibly. But you can imagine what conclusions would be drawn about this unfortunate young woman if it were known that a well-dressed gentleman was making enquiries about her whereabouts. And don't think it has escaped my attention that you have been champing at the bit to do something.'

Diana could not help giggling self-consciously at this. 'Oh, sir, you make me quite ashamed of how transparent I must appear to you.'

'Don't be. I find you — refreshing.'

Diana scrabbled about in her pocket and managed to find a visiting card, but she was forced to borrow a pencil from her companion so she could write down the address.

★ ★ ★

For once it worked in Diana's favour that her stepmother was already convinced of her flighty and inconsistent nature. Hence Mrs Aspley was bemused but not unduly surprised when Diana suggested that she needed a new evening gown and, moreover, that it should be made by a mantua-maker that Mrs Aspley had never heard of but who had apparently been recommended by an acquaintance, though Diana pretended to be unable to remember who that acquaintance might have been.

Mrs Aspley sighed her most exasperated sigh, and yet Diana suspected her stepmother was secretly pleased that she was apparently taking more interest in her appearance. Because did that not mean that maybe the tiresome girl was finally taking seriously the need to attract a suitable husband?

The deception and the expense of an unnecessary gown made Diana squirm, especially as she was sure her step-mother would not agree that the ends justified the means.

To try to compensate for her duplicity, Diana resolved to allow her stepmother to choose the material and the style of the gown, because she knew such occupations made Mrs Aspley happy.

Soho, Diana discovered, was a formerly fashionable part of London whose fortunes had declined as the aristocracy had moved westwards. A few old families, whose fortunes had declined likewise, still owned large houses there, but others were now occupied by the nouveau riche and up-and-coming tradesmen of the more respectable sort.

She was relieved to find Mrs Duberry's establishment looked respectable and prosperous from outside.

The lady herself, in a pristine black

silk gown, hurried to greet them and immediately dispatched an assistant to procure tea for the new clients, while the material Mrs Aspley had chosen was admired and the style of the gown was discussed. Despite her French-sounding name, the mantua-maker was clearly of native growth. Diana thought she even detected a hint of cockney beneath her carefully enunciated gentility.

But otherwise Diana was disappointed. The chief assistant quite plainly was not Alice, being small, plump and dark-haired, and the esteemed clients had been whisked into the mantua-maker's inner sanctum so quickly that Diana had barely glimpsed the workroom in which half-a-dozen seamstresses were at work, pinning patterns, cutting, sewing, pressing seams and whatever else it was that they did.

Mrs Duberry's Assistant

Diana was forced to wait until Mrs Duberry was showing them to the door and Mrs Aspley's back was turned towards her. There would never be a better opportunity than this.

'Is this where all the work takes place?' she exclaimed in her most child-like tone as they passed through the workroom. 'Do let me see.'

And before her stepmother could recover from her surprise, Diana had darted in among the tables at which the seamstresses sat. Several of the girls looked up, startled by this unexpected interruption, and then looked away, abashed and afraid of being chided for staring at the fine lady.

'Oh, what a beautiful sprigged muslin,' she continued, bending closer to admire the gown the nearest seamstress was sewing. 'I suppose it must be a very grand lady who has asked to have this made up for her. What style of sleeve has she ordered for it?'

The seamstress stammered a reply and spread out the gown to demonstrate, but she was interrupted by a sharp voice.

'Diana!'

There was a mingling of exasperation and bewilderment in Mrs Aspley's voice, since she had never seen her stepdaughter take so much interest in the cut of her own clothes, much less those of a stranger.

But Diana was not to be put off so easily.

'Coming in a moment,' she replied with her sweetest, most innocent smile.

And then, after a few more friendly words to the first seamstress, she moved on to the next, to admire her handiwork and ask her some random question.

And so she began to work her way round the room, while Mrs Aspley gazed on in astonishment. A covert glance at Mrs Duberry revealed to Diana that she was none too pleased to have her seamstresses interrupted in this manner, but of course she could not say anything to a valuable, if whimsical, new client.

Instead she suggested politely to Mrs Aspley that she too might like to inspect the quality of work produced in her workshop. Diana knew her stepmother would not be able to resist the temptation to examine other ladies' finery and maybe discover if any of it belonged to one of her acquaintances.

That made everything simpler for Diana. It had become clear to her fairly quickly that Alice was not present in the workroom, but she was loath to leave any stone unturned. After all, it was possible that Alice might simply have stepped out for a moment on an errand, or might be ill that day.

Diana chose a seamstress with a round, friendly face and a generously proportioned mouth, whom she suspected of being the boldest among the girls and the most inclined to gossip.

'I never realised there was such a lot of work involved in making a gown,' Diana remarked. 'You must get in one another's way from time to time.'

'Oh, we all have our jobs assigned to us, depending on how long we've been here and how skilled we are.' This was clearly the official reply rather than the true one.

'But still, there are — ' Diana counted rapidly — 'six of you in here. There must be some rivalries and jealousies, as well as friendships.'

'Ah well . . . ' The seamstress murmured and shrugged uncomfortably, confirming Diana's conjecture. 'Sometimes we get very busy and then tempers can become short.'

'And you have to do all the work between you?' Diana asked sympathetically. 'Is there nobody else to help out?'

'Mostly it's just us. But when we're really busy, at the beginning of the

Season or just before the King's birthday, Mrs Duberry pays some outside workers to do the plain sewing so we can do the more intricate work.'

'Oh?' Diana tried to sound casual, but her mind was working rapidly, trying to find some way she could ask after Alice and still make her question sound natural. But there didn't seem to be any other way to approach the matter apart from the most straightforward one. 'I don't suppose one of the outside workers might be a young, fair-haired widow with a baby?'

The round-faced seamstress had attempted to continue sewing throughout the previous conversation, but now she looked up, startled, and jabbed her finger. She uttered a cry, shook her hand and lifted the injured finger to her mouth to suck.

'Aye, there is one that fits that description, but . . . '

Diana produced a dazzling smile. 'A girl like that did some work for me a while ago,' she said. 'I was wondering where I might find her.'

But the seamstress shook her head.

'Couldn't tell you that, ma'am,' she said. 'We've little enough to do with the outside workers. They only come in to deliver finished wares and fetch new work.' She dropped her voice and glanced over her shoulder. 'And Mrs Duberry doesn't encourage chit-chat as a general rule.'

'No, of course not,' Diana replied, trying to hide her disappointment. To be so tantalisingly close, only for the thread to snap in her fingers like this.

How could she contrive another expedition to Mrs Duberry's shop? Mrs Aspley had arranged with the mantua-maker that she would deliver the gown directly to the townhouse and any further fittings that were required would take place there.

Moreover, the best hope of meeting Alice as if by chance would be during the next busy period in the social calendar. The King's birthday was not 'til early June and so Diana assumed the demand for new clothes for the occasion would not begin for some weeks yet.

It seemed a horribly long time to wait, and to leave a vast deal to chance. Who was to say that even if Diana did find an excuse to return to the shop that Alice would go there on the same day at the same hour?

All that Diana could resolve to do was talk to Mr Godolphin, though she suspected he might know even less than she did about the life and work of a casual seamstress.

She was jolted out of her brooding as something brushed against her.

'Oh, I beg your pardon, ma'am,' Mrs Duberry's assistant murmured, stooping to pick up the reels of thread she had dropped as the two of them collided.

'Oh, think nothing of it,' Diana said as she stooped to help the other girl.

The seamstress glanced up at her. Diana was quite taken aback by her penetrating look. Perhaps it was just that she was unused to a lady helping her like this.

'Did I hear right? Were you just asking about . . . ?' the seamstress began, but just at that moment, Diana heard her stepmother calling her.

Torn, she glanced at Mrs Aspley, then back at Mrs Duberry's assistant. But the latter's expression had changed from eagerness to studied neutrality.

'I'm coming,' Diana called over her shoulder, before turning back to the seamstress. 'Did you wish to ask me something?'

But the girl merely dropped her eyes and curtsied.

'No, ma'am,'

After that answer, there was nothing Diana could do apart from obey her stepmother's summons. But she couldn't quite repress the fizzle of excitement in her stomach, which fought with the cold, clear logic in her head. She had no absolute proof that the mantua-maker's assistant had overheard her conversation with the seamstress, nor that she had intended to tell her something about Alice.

And yet she couldn't quite repress her hope.

★   ★   ★

'Did I do well?'

Diana couldn't help herself. The words escaped her as she came to the conclusion of her account of her adventures at the mantua-maker's workshop.

A smile curled Mr Godolphin's lips and he flickered a glance at her.

'You are a minx of the first water,' he declared, 'but yes, you did admirably well in the circumstances.'

'And you do agree with me that Mrs Duberry's assistant must have known something and she would have told me if we had had the opportunity?' Diana persisted, still anxious for his approval.

'Well, obviously, I was not present at the time,' he replied. 'But from what you tell me, I believe your conjecture is correct.'

'And so I suppose when she comes with Mrs Duberry to try on the new gown, I shall have to find some excuse to speak to her alone.' Diana continued thinking out loud. 'Oh, what if Mrs Duberry comes alone or brings one of her other seamstresses with her?'

The very thought made Diana grip Mr Godolphin's arm in sudden panic. He turned grave eyes upon her.

'Miss Aspley,' he said, coolly and distinctly, 'it is far too soon to fret over such eventualities. If such a calamity were to strike, we would find some method to overcome it.'

Diana felt the panic ebbing from her under his steady gaze. She loosened her grip.

'Yes. Yes, of course.' But then, unable to help herself, she added, 'But what if . . .'

She got no further.

'Hush. No more. Unless you *want* to miss the spectacle?'

Diana subsided at this. It had been Mr Godolphin's suggestion that they

150

should come to Hyde Park to watch the military review and it was thanks to his foresight that they had managed to find such an advantageous spot from which to view the scene. Diana and her stepmother had walked hither, but Mrs Godolphin had played into their hands by suggesting that Diana might have a better viewpoint from her son's curricle and more protection from the sun from the vehicle's hood.

Never had she seen such a mass of scarlet coats, interspersed with the more colourful uniforms of the bandsmen. Buttons and weapons had been polished so they caught the sunlight.

Unconsciously she scrambled to her feet to get a better look, one hand instinctively gripping Mr Godolphin's shoulder for support when the carriage swayed beneath her while the other hand clung to her hat brim, to prevent the wind from flapping it into her face and obscuring her vision.

'Oh, aren't they magnificent?' she exclaimed. 'I wonder that the French have the temerity to face them on the battlefield at all.'

Mr Godolphin could not help laughing at that.

'I think you'll find the French army is equally well-disciplined,' he said.

'Oh, fie, what an unpatriotic thing to say,' Diana chided, but spluttering with laughter all the same.

And then somehow the laughter died on her lips as she found herself mesmerised by Edgar Godolphin's gaze. Time slowed. Nothing seemed to exist apart from those eyes.

Belatedly coming to her senses, she blushed, averted her face and, withdrawing her hand from his shoulder, she tucked herself demurely back into her seat. Mr Godolphin too stirred and cleared his throat, as if about to say something of grave importance. But if so, he never had the opportunity.

'Miss Aspley, how charming to see you again,' a masculine voice suddenly greeted her from somewhere to one side of Mr Godolphin's curricle. 'I daresay you don't remember me.'

Her eyes flew straight to the figure of an elegantly attired gentleman with one arm protectively bound up in a sling.

'Oh, Mr Beaumont.' She could not repress a smile of genuine pleasure. 'Of course I remember you. Never was I more shocked in my life than when I heard you had been injured in that dreadful duel.'

Mr Beaumont's expression darkened. Diana could have bitten her tongue out for being so tactless.

'Oh, I'm so sorry . . . ' she began at exactly the same moment that he too began to speak.

'I trust you did not believe any of the more shocking stories that were circulated at the time.'

'Oh no, of course not,' she replied. 'I was sure it must all have been . . . '

Beside her, Mr Godolphin uttered a low cough.

'Oh, how remiss of me,' Diana exclaimed. 'You remember Mr Godolphin, don't you?'

Mr Beaumont bowed.

'How could I possibly forget?'

The gentlemen exchanged greetings. However, Diana couldn't help noticing that Mr Godolphin's demeanour remained stiff and he merely nodded in response to Mr Beaumont's bow.

But after all, Diana chided herself, he *was* seated in a curricle. What else could he be expected to do? And the conversation that followed was perfectly civilised, if rather formal and distant, though not for want of effort on Mr Beaumont's part. He made certain that Diana too was included in the conversation, asking her what she had thought of the review and smiling indulgently at her enthusiasm.

When Mrs Aspley decreed it was time to reclaim her stepdaughter, Mr Beaumont was perfectly charming to her as well. He assisted Diana to alight from the curricle and offered to escort them home, when he discovered they were to make the journey on foot.

In contrast, Mr Godolphin continued

behaving in an oddly detached manner. Diana had just enough vanity to wonder whether her stepmother's assessment might be correct, only to dismiss it with a sigh.

* * *

Mrs Aspley would have been astonished if she had known how anxious Diana was for her new gown to be ready for its first fitting. On the morning that Mrs Duberry was due to call, she drove her stepmother to distraction by wandering about the drawing room, playing snatches of music on the piano or sewing a few untidy stitches before she was up and gazing out of the window once more.

When at last the hackney coach arrived bearing Mrs Duberry, the precious bandbox and the dark-haired seamstress, Diana could hardly refrain from dashing down the main staircase and flinging open the front door, instead of waiting for the seamstresses to be admitted by the tradesmen's entrance and then announced by one of the maids.

Diana felt tightly coiled, like a spring. She had no plan for how to proceed, though she had spent several nights trying to anticipate anything that might prevent her from talking to Mrs Duberry's assistant, whose name she didn't even know.

'Diana? What on earth is the matter with you?'

She had been standing by the window too long, she realised, while her stepmother had been talking to her, unheeded. Diana mustered a smile.

'Nothing,' she replied. 'I'm coming.'

Mrs Aspley insisted that they should all adjourn to her dressing room, since it had the best morning light and the handsomest pier-glass in the house. It was a room Diana had hardly ever set foot in and she was overwhelmed at first by the combined scent of her stepmother's perfume and the contents of various mysterious jars and bottles on the dressing table.

Diana succeeded in catching the eye of the younger seamstress as she slipped into the room, but the girl dropped her head modestly and seemed only concerned with unfastening the box that contained the precious new gown. But Mrs Duberry shooed her assistant aside as soon as the box was open.

'I'll see to this,' she said. 'You go and assist Miss Aspley.'

The eyes of the two younger women met fleetingly, but silently the seamstress set about helping Diana to unfasten and remove her gown. Mrs Duberry had taken the new gown by its shoulders and held it up so it unfurled and fell in graceful folds.

Mrs Aspley was cooing delightedly and Mrs Duberry demonstrating the fall of the sleeve or some such thing. The two of them could not have been more oblivious to what their younger subordinates were doing.

'I'm so glad you were the one who came with Mrs Duberry today,' Diana whispered to the seamstress. 'What should I call you? You did want to say something to me that day, didn't you?'

The seamstress blushed and stammered, hardly knowing which of Diana's questions to respond to first.

'I — well — I — '

'Oh, I'm sorry. Mrs Aspley is forever chiding for asking too many questions at once,' Diana went on, contrite. 'You heard me asking one of the other seamstresses about one of the outside workers, didn't you?'

But the seamstress cast an anxious look at her employer before she answered.

'You were the one who answered my advertisement, weren't you?'

The seamstress hesitated, then nodded.

'Trust me, I mean no harm,' Diana continued.

'Are you still not ready, Diana?'

Her stepmother's voice felt like a bucket of ice water flung in her face.

'Almost,' she replied, meekly enough,

though frustration boiled inside her.

There was no possibility of any more confidences as Mrs Duberry came to take charge. With the aid of her assistant, she lifted the new gown over Diana's head, manoeuvred her arms into the sleeves and tweaked the folds of the skirts.

'Oh, Diana.'

Mrs Aspley uttered such an unaccustomed, blissful little sigh that Diana suspected a hint of sarcasm. And then she turned and caught sight of herself in the mirror, flanked by the two seamstresses and her breath caught in surprise.

'Oh.'

For once, she was speechless. She knew she was tolerably pretty — her stepmother had told her so occasionally and sometimes she could not help being pleased with her reflection.

But this gown was completely different to her usual style. It made her look like a true lady, not a young hoyden, liable to lose her gloves, ladder her stockings and stain her fingers while out picking blackberries in the hedgerows near her home.

She scarcely even noticed Mrs Duberry fussing around her, though obediently she turned one way and the other so the others could decide whether the hem was the correct length or not. Diana was only awoken from her trance when Mrs Duberry decreed that the fitting was complete and Mary, as she referred to her assistant, should help her remove the new gown.

'Just a few more finishing touches before it will be all complete, I trust, to your satisfaction.'

The words meant little to Diana. She was more than satisfied with the dress already.

While Mrs Duberry carefully folded and put away the new gown, overseen by Mrs Aspley, who seemed still in its thrall, Mary gathered up Diana's ordinary morning dress. This, Diana reminded herself sternly, might be her last chance.

'The seamstress I'm looking for is a good friend of mine who has fallen upon hard times,' she whispered. 'I'd do anything to help her. So if you could tell me where I might find her I'd be enormously grateful.'

Mary did not reply. Instead she cast another glance at her employer and Diana's heart sank. It was no use. They were almost out of time. The girl didn't quite trust her.

And then Mary drew something surreptitiously from her apron pocket and, brushing lightly past her client, she slipped a piece of paper into Diana's hand.

'I copied it from Mrs D's ledger,' she whispered back. 'But if anything amiss happens, I had nothing to do with it.'

'Thank you, for everything.'

Diana was relieved that she could utter those words aloud, to encompass Mrs Duberry and even her stepmother who, between them, had created the glorious new gown. She could not look at Mary's note, though she managed to

161

tuck it inside her bodice while pretending to adjust the neckline of her dress.

'Well,' Mrs Aspley declared, once the seamstresses had been ushered down-stairs, 'if ever you remember who it was that recommended Mrs Duberry, you must be sure to thank her profusely. Quite a find.'

'Yes, I think so too,' Diana replied, hugging her secret to herself.

'Shall we repair to the drawing room?'

It was rare that Mrs Aspley was in such a genial mood with her stepdaugh-ter and Diana was loath to do anything that might jeopardise familial harmony. But she felt she might burst if she didn't glance at Mary's note and consign it to a better hiding place.

'You go ahead,' she said. 'There's something I want to fetch from my room.'

Diana had to draw in her breath before she could extract Mary's note from her bodice. Her fingers quivered as she unfolded it and smoothed out the creases.

It was just a name — Annie Smith — and an address in a street Diana had never heard of. But it was a start.

'I Must Speak To You'

That evening Diana and Mrs Aspley had been invited to a dinner party, which Edgar Godolphin had arranged as soon as he had been informed of the date of Mrs Duberry's call. But Diana's patience was put to the test once more. They were by no means the only guests and, as the host, Mr Godolphin was much in demand. Diana could not repress a flash of irritation. How could he look so serene while making polite conversation with his mother's friends, or bantering with the younger guests?

There was no opportunity for any private conversation at all before dinner. And afterwards Diana could barely prevent herself from squirming in her seat while the ladies waited for the gentlemen to join them.

Diana had given up hope and was gazing dismally at nothing when she heard a voice just behind her.

'Miss Aspley, I fear I have been neglecting you shamefully.'

There was something about Edgar Godolphin's tone that made Diana flush, as if he had meant something else entirely.

She wanted to stay cross with him, but she was not sure it was possible when he spoke so gravely while looking at her with such a twinkle in his eyes.

'Perhaps I haven't quite decided whether to forgive you or not,' she replied loftily.

He laughed as he sat down beside her.

'Then I shall presume upon your good nature and pretend that you have,' he said. 'I cannot imagine you holding a grudge.'

Diana tried to pout at that, but it was true. She had never been very good at sulking, even when she thought she had every right to feel slighted. And besides, she was aware that time was pressing and if she sparred him with him for too long, they might be interrupted.

They exchanged smiles and, having glanced round, Edgar Godolphin hitched his chair a fraction closer.

'So, have you discovered anything of interest?' he asked, dropping his voice to a confidential murmur.

'Well, there wasn't much opportunity to *talk*,' she replied, 'but . . . '

As if by accident, she allowed her handkerchief to drop. Mr Godolphin instantly leaned forward to retrieve it and fortunately was sharp-sighted enough to spot the fragment of paper that had fluttered to the floor too.

One swift look was exchanged, confirming his suspicions, and instantly the scrap of paper had been concealed in the breadth of his palm, while he returned the handkerchief to her with due ceremony.

'It's only a name and an address,' Diana went on. 'I don't even know if Annie Smith is someone who knows Alice, or the name she is currently using.'

'Assuming this is the correct woman.'

Perhaps Mr Godolphin saw that his caveat had crushed Diana, because he went on.

'What about the address?'

Diana shook her head.

'I don't know the street at all, or where it might be,' she said. 'I know I don't know London very well, but I'm afraid that, well, it might not be in a very nice area and it might be difficult to arrange a meeting.'

Involuntarily, she glanced towards her stepmother, who seemed to be discussing something with a good deal of animation with one of the older gentlemen. Turning back to Mr Godolphin, Diana noticed a pucker between his brows that suggested he was pondering the question.

'So,' she prompted him, 'what do we do next?'

Mr Godolphin shook his head.

'I don't know,' he said. 'We shall have to give it some thought.'

But there was no chance of that at

present as someone uttered his name and he was forced to resume his role of the perfect host.

* * *

He didn't come. Diana could not believe it. Even after the usual visiting hour was over, she remained in a state of shocked disappointment.

She had managed to convince herself during the wakeful hours of the night that Edgar Godolphin would certainly call the following morning, alone or with his mother.

It was an uncharacteristically bad-tempered Diana that sat down at her dressing table to prepare for an assembly that evening. She was in no mood for dancing or to make polite conversation with dull acquaintances.

Almost the first person to greet them at the door was Mr Beaumont. Diana mustered a smile, but as soon as her stepmother was otherwise engaged, the gentleman leaned closer so he could murmur, 'You seem in low spirits tonight, Miss Aspley.'

'Oh.' Taken aback, Diana hesitated between denying and acknowledging the truth of his statement. 'Well, perhaps, a little. But I'm sure it is nothing that some amusing company cannot cure.'

He smiled and bowed.

'I will do my utmost to oblige,' he replied. 'Do you suppose dancing might be a good cure too?'

'I think dancing might be the perfect cure.'

As she smiled and accepted his hand so he could lead her to the dance-floor, her eye was caught by a familiar figure at the far end of the crowded ballroom. Edgar Godolphin's face brightened as their eyes met, then darkened when he saw who her partner was.

But Diana only lifted her chin higher. What right had he to approve or disapprove of her dancing partners, when he had not had the courtesy to call on her when he *must* have known how desperate she was to talk to him?

This little spark of spirit enabled her to respond to Mr Beaumont when he teased and flirted with her while they were waiting for the music to begin. Diana unbent so much that it came as a shock when her partner winced as another dancer brushed past him too closely.

'Oh,' she murmured sympathetically, 'is your injury still giving you trouble?'

'It's nothing,' he said.

But the warm glow Diana had felt because he had done so much to cheer her was tainted by a spasm of guilt.

Conversation became impossible once they were moving. Moreover, to add to her difficulties, as she and Mr Beaumont cast down the set, she caught the eye of Mr Godolphin, who was just leading his partner up the set to meet them.

Something about the way he looked at her made Diana flush and avert her face, but it was only a temporary reprieve. As in most country-dances, she knew she would be obliged to dance with her corner as well as her partner.

Diana felt Mr Godolphin's gaze upon her face across the diagonal of their set of four while Mr Beaumont was setting and turning with Mr Godolphin's partner, a statuesque beauty whom Diana knew only by sight and not by name.

And then it was her turn. Diana lifted her chin as she setted to the right and the left, before Mr Godolphin offered both hands to her. He grasped her fingers more firmly than she had expected, subtly pulling her closer as they turned.

'I must speak to you,' he said.

She arched her eyebrows.

If they had been alone, she might have pointed out that he would have had ample opportunity to speak to her if he had called that morning.

It was a relief to progress one more place down the set, where she would not be so badly distracted by Mr

Godolphin. Even so, the memory of the clasp of his hands, his urgent whisper continued to haunt her, no matter how much Mr Beaumont tried to distract her.

There was scarcely time to catch breath until they had made their way to the foot of the set. Then Mr Beaumont took her by surprise again.

'I think I have discovered the cause of your low spirits.'

Diana jumped so violently that the fan with which she had been cooling her face slipped from her fingers. They both instinctively stooped to retrieve it, but Mr Beaumont reached it first. He looked up at her and there was something so intimate about his smile that Diana grew more hot and flustered than ever.

'Thank you,' she murmured.

'I am right, am I not?' he persisted. 'There has been some — misunderstanding between you and — a certain gentleman whose name begins with G?'

Diana flicked the fan open to conceal

as much of her face as she could.

'No, no, nothing like that, I assure you,' she replied, tempted once more to ignore Mr Godolphin's injunction and confide in him about Alice.

Before she could find the right way to broach the subject, her partner went on.

'Oh, come now, Miss Aspley, surely I have a right to know if you are dancing with me solely because you have had a lovers' quarrel with — '

Diana's explosive laugh cut him short. The sound echoed across the ballroom and she clapped her hand to her mouth, mortified.

'You are labouring under a delusion, sir,' she replied. 'Mr Godolphin is a family friend, no more than that.'

There wasn't time to analyse why her voice wobbled on the last words, as they were launched back into the dance.

Diana's emotions remained in turmoil as they made their way up the set, with each repetition growing closer and closer to Mr Godolphin.

This time she and Mr Godolphin were the first to set and turn. She tried to smile politely, but oh, it was hard, when he gazed at her with such a peculiarly intense stare. She could not repress the shiver that trickled down her spine as he clasped her hands.

Her heart was throbbing in anticipation, as well as from exertion, when at long last she found herself alone with Mr Beaumont at the top of the set. But all he did was smile a melancholy smile and sigh. Diana's heart melted.

'You sound very unhappy,' she said. 'Is dancing with me such an ordeal?'

Instantly his eyes were gazing deep into hers.

'Oh, no, Miss Aspley, you must never think so badly of me. I hold you in the highest esteem,' he said. 'It was just that seeing so many happy couples about us, some of them evidently in love, made me think of my own sad case and how impossible it is that I should ever . . . ' His voice broke and he was forced to stop.

Before she realised what she was doing, Diana discovered she had clasped Mr Beaumont's wrist.

'Perhaps things are not as hopeless as they appear to be at the moment.'

His eyes had been lowered, but now he raised them to her face. Diana could see incredulity battling with hope.

'Do you mean — no, you cannot possibly . . . '

How could Mr Godolphin possibly doubt him? He was clearly a man in love, unable to forget her, no matter how she had been led astray.

'I — well, I cannot say any more at present, but I would not wish you to despair just yet.'

She wanted to withdraw her hand, but suddenly Mr Beaumont was clasping it between both of his.

'God bless you, Miss Aspley,' he murmured in an impassioned undertone. 'You are an angel.'

'I hardly think my stepmother would agree with you on that score,' she replied, taking refuge in humour because the intensity of the conversation made her uncomfortable.

For the whole of their second dance, she managed to keep any more expressions of Mr Beaumont's gratitude at bay, by talking of inconsequential things.

But as soon as those first two dances were over, Diana grew restless again. Mr Beaumont was apparently engaged for the next dances and therefore obliged to leave her.

'At last,' Mr Godolphin said. 'I thought I would never be able to speak to you.'

'A pity you did not call upon me this morning.' Diana knew she ought to let go of the grudge, but she had been holding the words in for too long.

'I was busy this morning. I've found her,' he said.

Finding Annie Smith

The whole world seemed to stand still for a moment longer. Then there was a stir as a dozen other couples began to move towards the dance-floor.

'How? Where? How is she?' Diana asked in a whisper.

'We should go if we intend to dance,' Mr Godolphin said.

'Oh, you cannot keep me in suspense like this.' Diana barely prevented herself from stamping her foot.

'We must maintain appearances,' Mr Godolphin replied, offering her his hand. 'You do realise we are already being talked about.'

Diana flushed. The thought of Edgar Godolphin as a suitor, possibly even as a husband made her dizzy.

'Tell me one thing,' she pleaded. 'Does she look well?'

He looked at her from beneath hooded eyelids.

'She seems well enough, though I'm no great judge of such things,' he replied. 'I suppose I ought to tell you that I went this morning to the address you gave me. I'd no intention of doing anything more than observe the place, but as I was about to leave, a fair-haired woman came out of the house, carrying a baby.'

'You talked to her?' Diana felt a bubble of joy catch in her throat.

'Not at first. I followed her at a distance, wanting to see where she would go. Then two urchins dashed past her and knocked her basket out of her hands, and what else could I do but go to her assistance?'

Diana could imagine the scene perfectly. Alice flustered and grateful; Mr Godolphin the model of gentlemanly politeness. The inevitability of conversation between them.

'I had had my doubts before then if I was even following the right woman,' he went on, 'but she looks like your sketches and her voice was far too genteel for someone born to her current lowly station in life.'

'So what did you say to her? Did you tell her I was looking for her?'

'I didn't want to alarm her, so I couldn't exactly interrogate her. She was on her way to deliver some work to an employer — I gather she works for more than one seamstress — but the topmost garment had tumbled out into the mud and naturally she was upset because she feared she would lose her pay if the work was late or dirty. So I said I'd go with her to explain to her employer and offer to pay for the damage.'

He spoke the words unwillingly, not meeting her eye, as if he feared she would think he was bragging about his act of kindness.

'I cannot be sure what the mantua-maker did once I was gone, but she sounded conciliatory enough to my face. At any rate, I gave Mrs Smith my card and told her she was to come to me if she ever had any difficulty and that I knew some ladies who might be able to make use of her skills with the needle.'

'So, how can we arrange to meet her?' Diana asked. She had a few qualms about how easy it would be to persuade her stepmother to do anything she didn't want to do.

'Well,' Mr Godolphin said slowly, 'unless you have a better suggestion, I thought I would mention to my mother that I have met a suitable object for her charity. And then I might suggest that you and your stepmother might like to come with us to visit her.'

Diana could see the advantages instantly. The meeting would appear to be purely accidental. And Mrs Godolphin's presence would soften Mrs Aspley's shock at being brought face to face to Alice once more.

'You've thought of everything,' Diana said, squeezing Mr Godolphin's hand fervently. 'I can't thank you enough.'

'That's what friends are for.'

'Friends?' she echoed, then mustered her brightest smile.

But why was it that she felt something die within her?

No, she would not dwell on such things. Alice had been found. Perhaps as soon as tomorrow they would be reunited. And Mr Godolphin had professed to be her friend. Surely that was better than being 'the child'?

Things didn't go quite as smoothly as Diana had hoped. There was another day's delay, since she was obliged to receive her dancing partners the following morning. Mr Godolphin put the visit to good use, however, by telling Mrs Aspley about his mother's latest protégée, though he also frustrated Diana's attempts to enlighten Mr Beaumont.

But after all, Diana consoled herself, one more day could make little difference to a man so devoted to his true love.

After another night of veering between

wild hope and crippling doubt, Diana woke late and had to scramble through the process of getting dressed in time for breakfast. She didn't want anything to impede the unfolding of Mr Godolphin's plan.

So absorbed was Diana in her mission that she didn't see the figure loitering by the railings in front of the house, until a voice spoke to her while she was waiting to be helped into the coach.

'Miss?'

Diana blinked twice before she recognised Mrs Jones.

'Oh, it's you. How are the children? I hope Cook has given you whatever she can spare.' Diana rattled on much too fast, conscious that her stepmother could not help but overhear.

'The children are well enough and I've no complaints about your generosity, but,' Mrs Jones glanced significantly towards the carriage.

'Good, good. Excellent.'

Diana felt bad for dismissing her so

brusquely, but there really was no time for any more. She was conscious that her stepmother was regarding her sternly through the coach window, though she was obviously reserving whatever she had to say about being over-familiar with vagabonds until they were alone.

But Mrs Jones persisted.

'There's something I must speak to you about.'

Diana was torn. What should she do?

'Some other time.'

'But, Miss . . . '

'I cannot possibly . . . '

'Do you need any assistance?' Mr Godolphin intervened, stepping forward to shield Diana. He eyed Mrs Jones coolly.

'Oh no, no, it's — there's nothing to fret about. Do let's go.' Diana felt wretched about the whole business. Had she put Mrs Jones to a great deal of trouble and all to no good purpose, now that Mr Godolphin had found Alice?

For a second, from the look in the old woman's eyes, Diana was terrified that Mrs Jones would insist on saying whatever she had come to say, irrespective of who might be listening. Instead she dropped back two steps and Mr Godolphin did his duty by handing Diana into the coach. He threw one more glance at Mrs Jones, but at the urging of Mrs Aspley, he clambered in without uttering another word.

'I suppose you have been encouraging that woman, Diana?' Mrs Aspley asked, confounding her stepdaughter's expectations.

Diana wanted with all her heart to defend Mrs Jones, but she knew that, in the circumstances, she would only get herself into trouble if she did. So she dropped her head and allowed her stepmother to draw her own conclusions. She had the uncomfortable feeling, however, that Edgar Godolphin had given her a sidelong look.

The street to which the carriage took them was humble enough, narrow, dark and dirty, but not as bad as Diana had feared it might be, having heard horror stories from her acquaintances.

Perhaps Edgar Godolphin felt her tremor of anticipation as he helped her out of the coach, because he squeezed her fingers and smiled encouragingly when she glanced up at him. The ground floor of the house he led them into was taken up by a chandler's shop and they were forced to climb up two flights of increasingly dingy stairs to reach the attic floor.

There, Mr Godolphin rapped lightly at one particular door. It was enough to cause a baby to begin to wail.

'Good morning, Mrs Smith,' he said, doffing his hat and tucking it under his arm. 'I hope we did not disturb you or your daughter.'

'Oh no, not at all,' a slightly husky voice replied politely, though perhaps not entirely truthfully. 'Do come in.'

Diana deliberately hung back in an attempt not to look too eager. She kept her eyes fixed upon Mrs Aspley's back, expecting a start of recognition. But none came.

Unable to contain her impatience any longer, Diana slipped into the garret, dodging round the two older ladies so she could get her first proper glimpse of the seamstress. Her breath caught. The woman's head was lowered over the fretful baby. A wing of fair hair was visible beneath her widow's cap. And then she raised her head.

It was Diana who jumped. She found herself staring at Mrs Smith, who was exchanging pleasantries with the older ladies. Her eyes were the right shade of blue; her eyelashes long and black; her nose sweetly upturned. Almost every feature was right. And yet she was not Alice.

Moreover Diana was aware that Mr Godolphin's eyes were flitting between her, Mrs Aspley and Annie Smith, observing their reactions. It was all Diana could do not to cry in disappointment.

Mr Godolphin managed to catch her

eye and silently she shook her head. She could see from his expression that he had already suspected that something was wrong, but at this confirmation, his shoulders seemed to slump and he averted his face to try to conceal the darkening of his eyes.

It was as well that neither Mrs Godolphin nor Mrs Aspley seemed to notice anything amiss. Diana took refuge in silence. She gathered from the conversation that Annie Smith really was a widow who had fallen upon hard times because her parents had disapproved of her marrying a soldier, who had been killed during the retreat to Corunna.

Diana was aware that Mr Godolphin kept looking at her, as if he would have liked to speak to her, but there was no opportunity to do so without being overheard.

It was decided between the others that it was far too pleasant a day to waste indoors and that instead of returning straight home, they ought to take a stroll in one of the Royal Parks. The coach had almost reached their destination when Mr Godolphin suddenly sat forward.

'Would you have any objection if we were to stop here a moment? I need to buy some writing paper.'

Naturally all the ladies concurred. It was also agreed that since it was just a step from the bookseller's shop to Green Park, they might as well dismiss the carriage and walk the remainder of the way.

The shop was bustling and it was some time before Edgar Godolphin could be served. But there was plenty to keep all three ladies occupied while they waited. In addition to glancing over the newest novels, Diana also found herself observing some of the other customers. One woman in particular caught her eye because she did not seem to belong in this shop. She had sharp, hungry features, though she was dressed respectably enough, as if she might be a shopkeeper or an artisan's wife.

But, after all, Diana chided herself, why shouldn't a poor woman try to better herself by reading, if she had time, money and inclination?

She jumped at a voice close beside her.

'I cannot apologise enough for the disappointment you must have suffered this morning,' Edgar Godolphin said. 'I was convinced I had found the right woman.'

He looked so contrite that Diana's heart squeezed tightly in her chest. On impulse she touched his arm.

'It doesn't matter. It was an easy mistake to make. Mrs Smith really does look a lot like Alice.'

The four of them left the shop and had reached Green Park when Edgar drew Diana further ahead.

'I wanted to speak to you alone.'

Diana had been chattering vaguely about nothing in particular, but his abrupt words brought her to a halt.

Diana's heart began to palpitate. The

rustic setting of the park, the meaningful glances of the chaperones, the distance Edgar Godolphin had made sure he had placed between them and the older ladies . . . surely, it couldn't be what she thought.

He cleared his throat uncomfortably.

'I wasn't sure if I ought to bring this up after this morning's disappointment,' he went on. 'I would be loath to raise false hopes again.'

Diana felt her heart plummet. False hopes. Yes, she had been toying with those, though not of the kind he meant.

'I — I don't understand,' she faltered.

'There was another note left for you this morning at the bookseller's shop.'

'For me?' Her mind did not seem to want to work fast enough. 'Oh, you mean in reply to the advertisement?'

He glanced down at her.

'Yes.'

'Then it isn't all over yet. There's still a chance . . . '

Diana felt excitement stir inside her,

despite her previous disappointment. She peered over her shoulder to see how large the gap between them and their chaperones had grown by now.

'You really are irrepressible,' Edgar Godolphin replied and even without seeing his expression, Diana could hear the smile in his voice.

By chance, she caught sight of a solitary figure on a parallel path. It was the same woman she had noticed in the bookseller's shop. There was something about the intent way she was staring at Mr Godolphin that arrested Diana's gaze. The woman stared back and Diana looked away first, abashed.

She was wondering if she ought to point the woman out to Mr Godolphin, when he spoke.

'Perhaps you ought to open the note now.' He threw a swift look around, then extracted a tightly folded rectangle of paper from his glove and slipped into her hand.

Diana did as she was bid and could not repress a cry of surprise. A curl of blonde hair, tied with forget-me-not blue thread slid out of the package. Only a few words were printed on the single sheet of paper in green ink.

Vauxhall Pleasure Gardens, Friday night, 9 o'clock at the cascade.

Vauxhall Pleasure Gardens

'What is it?' Diana was vaguely aware that it was not the first time Edgar Godolphin had asked that question. Unable to speak, she slipped the note back to him, while retaining hold of the fair curl of hair.

'It's ambiguous enough,' Edgar Godolphin remarked, breaking her reverie.

'It's from her. I know it is.'

'Really? You recognise the handwriting, or the lock of hair?'

'No, it's the thread. She gave me forget-me-nots. We . . . ' It sounded so inadequate when spoken out loud, but Diana could feel conviction growing inside her.

'The *thread?*' He made no attempt to hide his incredulity. 'Pardon me, but are you not clutching at straws here?'

'You told me once to trust my instincts.'

'Not about something as nebulous as this. Have you ever been at the cascade in Vauxhall Gardens at nine? The only thing that is likely to happen there is that you will have your pocket picked while you are admiring the illuminations.'

Diana flushed. Suddenly she was forcibly reminded of the rough way in which Mr Godolphin had dragged her back to the hackney coach after she had run off in pursuit of Alice. It brought out a stubborn streak in her.

'I intend to ask my stepmother to take me there,' she said defiantly.

Edgar Godolphin tried to stare her down, but was forced to blink first. He turned his head away from her.

'Even if Miss Simmonds came in person, do you really think she would dare approach you while you were in the company of Mrs Aspley? Trust me, this is the work of law students playing a prank — or of some more sinister gang wanting to take advantage of your gullibility.'

'I am *not* gullible,' she retorted indignantly.

'Aren't you? So what proof do you have that this letter is genuine? Even that lock of hair might belong to a guttersnipe, or a woman of the streets.'

Diana found herself wavering, in spite of her best efforts.

'But suppose this is genuine. Suppose Alice comes and I am not there.' She surprised herself by suddenly uttering a sob and she blinked fiercely to bring herself back under control. 'Can't you see that if I don't go, I will always wonder whether I didn't miss my last opportunity to find her?'

Diana gazed earnestly at his profile, but then a cheerful voice cut in first.

'Here we are again.' Mrs Godolphin beamed at them. 'I hope you had a pleasant walk.'

Her son raised his head and from somewhere produced a brittle, brilliant smile.

'Delightful,' he said. 'So much so that I propose we should all go to Vauxhall together on Friday.'

Diana was aware that under any other circumstances, she would have enjoyed her first visit to Vauxhall Pleasure Gardens more than she did.

The long, tree-lined avenues, the octagonal bandstand and the curving colonnades of supper-boxes on either side of the central piazza ought to have excited her admiration or at least engaged her interest. Instead she found herself distracted and hardly able to pay attention to the conversations that were taking place around her.

'Don't worry, Miss Aspley,' a deep voice beside her interrupted her thoughts. 'You are in no danger of missing the cascade. It is announced every night by the ringing of a bell and some minutes before then the crowds will start moving in that direction.'

Diana flushed, hating to think that she was so transparent, but before she could think of some dignified retort, Mrs Godolphin intervened.

'Oh yes, you must not miss the cascade,' she said. 'It is quite a wonder, in particular for those who are here for the first time, though I must admit I never tire of it myself. My son, of course, thinks me an old fool, to be enchanted by such childish tricks.'

Edgar Godolphin denied this vehemently as a slur on his character and Diana mustered a smile, though she could still feel the flutter of nerves in the pit of her stomach.

It was only as their party was beginning to make its way along one of the alleys, beneath the widely spaced triumphal arches, that Edgar Godolphin succeeded in putting a slight distance between himself and Diana and their respective mothers.

'I suppose I ought to have thanked you for inviting us tonight,' Diana said stiffly.

Mr Godolphin cast her a sidelong look.

'I could not very well let you come on your own, with only your stepmother to protect you from — well, I hardly know what myself,' he replied.

Diana was torn between irritation because he seemed to think she was so incapable of looking after herself, and relief that he was there because, much though she would have hated to admit it, she was a little apprehensive.

'Of course, you do realise that this may prove to be a hoax and that we might meet nobody tonight,' he went on.

'Of course.' Diana tilted her chin higher. That possibility had been preying on her mind during the past few days.

There was a further complication when they reached the end of the avenue. Diana had assumed they would have to remain on the edge of the crowd so as to be more visible to anyone who intended to approach them. But their chaperones had caught up with them and Mrs Godolphin was determined that, since it was her first visit, Diana should have as good a view as possible. She jostled her way through the crowd, towing Diana along behind her, with Edgar Godolphin and Mrs Aspley trailing in their wake.

She glanced up at Edgar Godolphin, silently pleading with him to think of something, but he seemed unconcerned, as if he was relieved at being offered this way out of an awkward situation.

In any case, it was too late. The bell rang, a watchman called out, 'Take care of your pockets' and the show began.

A curtain was whisked aside to reveal a model of a rustic scene, complete with a watermill. The cascade itself was made of strips of tin and when the concealed lights played upon it, it shimmered and seemed to ripple, like a genuine millrace. Diana found herself distracted by the spectacle, though she knew she ought to be watching the crowd surreptitiously.

'Pretty sight, ain't it, sir?' a woman's voice spoke on the other side of Mr Godolphin.

'Yes,' he replied briefly.

'The young lady as lodges with us, she said it was a sight worth seeing,' the woman persisted and Diana felt a dart of electricity shoot through her.

Alice had described the cascade in one of her letters from London the previous spring. Mr Godolphin had turned his head sharply towards the stranger.

'That's why I came here tonight,' the woman persisted, though she glanced nervously over her shoulder. 'On account of the lady — very sweet-natured, sir, but so unfortunate in her circumstances . . .'

Diana could not restrain herself any longer. 'Oh, that sounds exactly like . . .'

She stopped with a gasp because Mr Godolphin had turned towards her so sharply that his frown made her heart hammer in her breast.

'I'd do a deal, sir, miss, to see our lodger safe back with her friends,' the woman's voice went on. 'She ain't fit for the life she's leading now — a deal too delicately born.'

This time all of Mr Godolphin's stern looks could not restrain Diana. She took a step forward so she could peep round him and get a clearer view of the woman.

'Are you the one who sent the letter?' she asked.

The stranger smiled, but the lights of the cascade cast eerie shadows across her face. Diana shivered.

'Aye, miss, and the lock of hair too. Couldn't we talk somewhere else, sir, more private?'

Mr Godolphin cast a single look past Diana to make sure his mother and her stepmother were still absorbed by the spectacle. Then he began to thread his way through the throng after the stranger. Diana was forced to cling to his arm, terrified of being separated from him in the crowd.

As they passed beneath one of the lanterns that illuminated the avenue, Diana caught a better look at the stranger's face. There was something familiar about her.

The woman led the way towards one of the narrower alleys that branched off the main avenue into the densely planted trees, but Edgar Godolphin stopped abruptly.

'This is quite private enough, in my opinion,' he said.

The woman murmured a protest, but quickly subsided when the gentleman remained adamant. Diana could not understand why Mr Godolphin was being so curt towards someone who was evidently trying to help.

His attitude seemed to unnerve the woman too. She licked her lips and glanced around as if she was afraid of being overheard even here. Diana's heart went out to her.

'Where is your lodger?' she asked. 'Is she well? Don't worry, you've nothing to fear from either of us,' she added, throwing a reproachful look at Mr Godolphin.

'Oh, bless your kind heart, miss, I

knew *you'd* never do nothing to harm me or anyone else. Miss Smith, that's the name she calls herself, she told me she had a good friend who'd do anything she could to help her.'

Diana's last doubts about the stranger fled. Her mysterious lodger simply could not be anyone other than Alice.

'So where is Miss Smith?' Mr Godolphin cut in.

The woman glanced from him to Diana, evidently looking for sympathy.

'Well, sir, she did want to come herself, except she was afraid it might be a trick by her seducer to lure her back into his clutches. And then when she took sick . . . '

'Alice is ill?' Diana exclaimed. 'But when I saw her a few weeks ago . . . '

'Oh, it came on very sudden,' the woman interrupted her. 'Indeed I had to call the apothecary in to see what he could do for her and my husband was so angry at the expense . . . '

Diana couldn't prevent a cry of

dismay from escaping her and she clutched Mr Godolphin's arm tighter. He placed his free hand on top of hers, as if to console her, or maybe to warn her not to say any more.

'Naturally any expenses you have incurred will be reimbursed — once we have ascertained that your lodger is indeed the person we seek,' he replied with a touch of irony.

'Oh, sir, I'm sure I wasn't hinting at any such thing, though I admit we're not well-off and I wouldn't say no to . . . well, never mind about all that now.'

'Oh, so this is where you've been hiding yourself, is it?' a deeper, rougher voice interrupted them. 'What the devil do you mean by it, getting me to take you to this confounded expensive place and then running away from me?'

Diana turned to face the newcomer, instinctively interposing herself between him and the woman to protect the latter. The man was almost as tall as Mr Godolphin and more broad-shouldered. Diana formed the impression he was the sort of man who would not be shy about using his fists if he felt the occasion warranted it. He was, however, dressed in what Diana assumed must be his Sunday coat in order to look respectable enough to be allowed through the gates of the pleasure garden.

'Please, Mr B, mind your language,' the woman stammered. 'The gentle-folks . . . '

'I'll use whatever language I choose to me own wife,' Mr B growled back.

'I wouldn't advise you to raise your voice too much,' Mr Godolphin intervened, as calmly as if he had made a remark on the weather. 'There are stewards about this place who are only too pleased to eject anyone who seems likely to cause a disturbance.'

Both women gasped. Diana felt her heart pounding suffocatingly in her breast. Was Mr Godolphin trying to provoke this man into a fight?

But though Mr B glared at him and his hands doubled into fists, he made no move towards Mr Godolphin. Mrs B hastily intervened.

'Please, Mr B, these are Miss Alice's friends,' she stammered.

'Oh, they are, are they? Well, did you tell 'em how much out of pocket we are because of you and your ways, eh? Did you tell 'em about the food and the medicine and the 'pothecary, never mind you rashly giving away our rent money to save her from being dragged off to debtors' prison?'

Diana let out another horrified cry at the thought of Alice being reduced to such straits. Mrs B was crying now and Diana put her arms around the other woman to comfort her. She couldn't understand how Mr Godolphin could remain so cool and detached. Her own mind was working frantically, trying to find a way to repay Alice's debts because she could not possibly allow strangers to suffer such financial loss.

'Oh, Mr B, how can you talk so?' Mrs B spluttered between her sobs. 'You can't just go around asking rich folks for money . . . '

'Why not? They've got it to spare and we've never enough, no matter how hard I work.' Mr B turned a somewhat belligerent look on Mr Godolphin, as if defying him to deny the truth of this.

But Mr Godolphin seemed coolly unimpressed by all this bluster.

'I'll make sure you are recompensed,' Diana intervened, but her voice was drowned out.

'Well,' Mr Godolphin said, 'edifying though this little scene has been, I have better things to do with my time.' The sarcasm in his drawl was too obvious to be ignored. 'Come along, child.'

Diana gasped, simultaneously outraged by the way he had addressed her and the lack of ceremony with which he seized her hand. Worst of all, after all their efforts to find Alice, she could not believe that he would walk away like this in a fit of pique.

'Oh, please, sir, don't go,' Mrs B called out in a heartbroken tone. 'My husband's a little rough-spoken, but he means no disrespect . . . '

She stopped abruptly as Edgar Godolphin turned his sternest look upon her.

'You know where to send a message to me as soon as Miss Smith is well enough to receive visitors,' he clipped.

And with that he turned on his heel and dragged Diana away after him.

Doubts and Disagreements

It took Diana a minute or so to recover, by which time they were out of sight and earshot of the other couple.

'Was it necessary to be so rude?' she demanded, wrenching herself free of Mr Godolphin's grip and whisking round to face him. 'Can't you see Mrs B is a good, Christian woman who has risked her own security to help someone in need? She deserves to be rewarded for her good works, not . . . '

'Does she? What makes you think she or her husband have ever met Miss Simmonds?'

For a moment Diana was left open-mouthed, trying to gather her scattered thoughts.

'What on earth do you mean? Of course they've met Alice. Didn't you hear what Mrs B said — that they've taken in a delicate, sweet-natured lady who has been seduced by some villain . . . '

'All of which she could easily have deduced from the advertisement in the newspaper,' Edgar interrupted her.

'She knew Alice's name.'

'No, *you* told her that. She called her Miss Smith, while implying she believed it was an alias.'

Diana could feel her arguments crumbling, but still she didn't want to let go of the hope that she might have found Alice.

'What about Alice telling them that she had a close female friend?'

'An intelligent guess, based on your impassioned reaction. Mrs B did not seem to know *your* name, did she?'

She turned away, wanting to escape from Edgar and yet knowing she could not do so unless she found her stepmother.

'And let me ask you this, Miss Aspley,' the inexorable voice went on beside her. 'Why was no mention made of the baby?'

Diana stopped in her tracks. Her mind whirred.

'They could have argued that the baby caused additional expense and trouble, with all the tending and the washing and the sleepless nights a small child causes. It would have added to the pathos of their story if they had saved not one, but two, unfortunate innocents from the jaws of debtors' gaol. Nothing appeals to the human heart more than an infant in distress, even an illegitimate one. I would not be surprised if that quarrel between them was deliberately staged to make you pity Mrs B and prevent you from thinking clearly enough to see through their deception.'

'No,' Diana cried out. 'I don't believe that . . .'

But her words were cut short by another voice.

'There you are,' Mrs Godolphin exclaimed. 'Wherever have you been hiding? Mrs Aspley was quite beside herself, though I told her you would look after Miss Aspley.'

She twinkled cheerfully at her son and seemed not to notice that his smile was a touch acidic.

Diana was startled to discover they had acquired an additional member to their party. Mr Beaumont might have had a lady on each arm, but his gaze was fixed ardently, questioningly, on Diana's face, as if he suspected that something was going on. Perhaps he had even overheard a fragment of her quarrel with Mr Godolphin. But under Diana's gaze, he dropped his eyes.

'I am sorry if we alarmed you,' Edgar Godolphin was saying. He inclined his head politely towards Mrs Aspley in particular. 'Miss Aspley felt a little faint in the press of the crowd and I thought it wiser to take her to a quieter spot.'

Diana felt a sudden rush of outrage. She had never been one of those delicate females who professed to feel faint at the slightest excuse in order to demonstrate their sensibility.

Hot words were already forming on

her lips. Then she caught Mr Godolphin's eye and the words died. What other excuse could she give for their absence?

Nonetheless Mrs Godolphin's sympathetic coos made Diana uncomfortable and she felt a flash of irritation when her stepmother threw her a knowing look, as if she thought Diana had finally taken her strictures to heart and started to play the role of defenceless female to try to ensnare the eligible Mr Godolphin.

'I am sure a little light refreshment would revive Miss Aspley completely,' Mr Beaumont intervened, but the smile he gave Diana suggested that he did not believe Mr Godolphin's excuse for a second. 'Would you do me the honour of accepting my arm to lean upon?'

Mr Godolphin uttered a sound that seemed to be a cross between a cough and a cry of protest, but Diana chose to ignore him.

'You are most kind, sir,' she replied, slipping her hand through the crook of

Mr Beaumont's arm. But she couldn't resist casting a defiant look back at the other gentleman.

For the remainder of the evening, Diana kept Edgar Godolphin at arm's length by devoting herself to Mr Beaumont. The latter gentleman was perfectly obliging and Diana's mood was only spoilt after they had returned to the townhouse, when her stepmother scolded her for behaving in a capricious, even coquettish fashion.

'I never believed you were the sort of girl who would toy with one man's feelings in order to make another one jealous.'

The encounter in Vauxhall Pleasure Gardens also preyed upon her mind during the night. Who was she meant to believe? Was Mr Godolphin right in thinking Mr and Mrs B were a pair of fraudsters, intent on milking her for as much money as they could get? Or had he frightened away the only people who could have helped her find Alice?

The worst of it was that she had

nobody to talk to. She knew her stepmother would not understand how she felt; her father was dead and she didn't feel close enough to any of her new acquaintances to tell them the full story. That left only Mr Godolphin and she was not at all sure his advice would be impartial or correct.

Her spirits had not improved by the following morning when Mrs Aspley insisted on dragging her off on a shopping expedition. Normally Diana had no particular objection to shopping, even with her stepmother. She was not the kind of girl to whom fashion was the most important thing in the world, but she liked to be out and about, seeing new things, meeting friends or acquaintances or even complete strangers, and maybe encountering some small adventure or odd incident.

But today her head ached from lack of sleep and her heart was heavy. She was not quite sure what prompted her to raise her head as she stepped out onto the steps leading down from the front door. Her eye was caught by a figure on the opposite side of the square. Involuntarily she gasped.

'What is it now, Diana?'

Ignoring her stepmother's exasperated question, Diana dashed down the steps, out through the wrought-iron gate and across the street, without even glancing left or right to see if there was any traffic approaching.

The woman had turned away as soon as she realised Diana had seen her, but she had not gone far, as if she was still hesitating between staying and going. Diana had no difficulty in catching up with her and grasping her arm.

As Mrs B turned her pinched features towards her, Diana realised suddenly where she had first seen her. She was the woman who had been in the bookseller's shop and in Green Park on the day Mr Godolphin had received the letter containing the lock of fair hair. All Diana's doubts fled in an instant.

'Oh, I am glad I caught up with you,'

she gasped,. 'How is Alice? She's not worse, is she?'

Her heart plummeted as Mrs B dropped her head and began to pleat the edge of her apron.

'Well, she — she's not well,' Mrs B admitted. 'I had to ask a neighbour to sit with her while I slipped out to carry out my errands — and to see you, Miss Aspley.'

Diana felt a surge of vindication. There, Mrs B *did* know her name and that information surely could only have come from Alice.

'But then I wasn't sure if you'd agree to see me and ... ' Mrs B's voice trailed away.

'Of course I wanted to see you. I was in despair, not knowing where to send for you, or even your name,' Diana replied.

'It's Brown, Miss. Plain Martha Brown,' the woman faltered. 'As to Miss Smith — '

'Oh, I do so wish I could go and visit her.' Diana could not help butting in.

'Nay, Miss. I'm not sure she's well enough for visits,' Mrs Brown replied. 'And I should never forgive myself if you was to be taken sick too.'

'But there must be something I can do,' Diana urged, instinctively searching for her purse and bitterly regretting the fripperies she had wasted her money on before she discovered that Alice was alive and in need. 'I don't have a vast deal to spare, but . . . '

'Oh, Miss Aspley, I couldn't possibly take it,' Mrs Brown murmured, taking the golden guinea Diana pressed into her hand all the same.

'It's the least I can do,' Diana insisted. 'Perhaps you could use it to pay the apothecary or buy some wholesome food to speed Alice's recovery, or — '

'Diana, who is this person?'

Mrs Aspley's voice made them both start. Diana had almost managed to forget that such a person existed, let alone was bound to follow her and disapprove of the way she had dashed off. Then Diana lifted her chin. Even with Edgar Godolphin as a half-unwilling ally, she had always known she would have to confess to her stepmother what she had done, since she was not financially independent and would need Mrs Aspley's help to assist Alice.

'Mrs Brown has been taking care of Alice,' she declared, throwing caution to the wind.

She saw the spasm of shock cross Mrs Aspley's face. Diana plunged on recklessly before her stepmother could utter a word.

'She's very ill, dying maybe. Surely you have enough compassion not to leave my poor friend to die amid strangers when maybe a little help from us could save her?'

But Mrs Aspley's expression was only growing more forbidding. Mrs Brown made a move as if she wanted to apologise and escape.

'Diana, really,' Mrs Aspley began with an exasperated sigh.

'Mr Godolphin approves. He's been helping me to search for Alice,' Diana cut in, ignoring the inconvenient fact that the first statement might not strictly be true.

She could see that her stepmother was uncomfortable that this conversation was taking place in front of the windows of all their neighbours. There was no telling how many people might be watching.

'I think we ought to discuss this indoors,' she said in frigid tones intended to repress any exuberance or defiance in her stepdaughter. 'And I shall send for Mr Godolphin too, to get to the bottom of this matter.'

Diana felt her heart sink, but she did not protest. Even if Mr Godolphin contradicted her on certain details, surely it was better for everything to be out in the open?

Mrs Brown started murmuring excuses about not being fit company for such grand folks and having to leave, but Diana caught hold of her arm and drew her along with them to the house.

'No, no, you cannot go yet,' Diana said. 'You must tell my stepmother all you have done to help my friend, despite being so poorly off yourself.'

'Oh, Miss, you'll put me to the blush,' the older woman mumbled as Diana ushered her up the steps and into the house. 'I only did what anyone else would've done in the same circumstances.'

Diana saw her stepmother bristle, as if she felt her charitableness was being compared unfavourably with that of someone who was quite clearly her inferior as far as wealth and rank were concerned.

Mrs Aspley led the way into the library where she scribbled a hasty note to Edgar Godolphin and despatched it via the hackney coach that was to have taken them to Oxford Street.

The wait seemed uncomfortably long. At Diana's prompting, Mrs Brown murmured a few sentences about taking a liking to the quiet, lady-like young woman who had been living in the room next door to her own and interceding on her behalf when the landlord had wanted to throw her out or have her arrested when she couldn't pay her rent.

But clearly Mrs Aspley's haughty presence was making her uncomfortable.

'I really should be going soon,' Mrs Brown murmured. 'I can't expect my neighbour to spend all day caring for my patient after all.'

Diana was half-inclined to let her go, but at that moment a sharp rattle at the doorknocker heralded the arrival of Edgar Godolphin. Mrs Brown cast a wistful look at the window, as if she would have bolted if she could.

'Ah, Mr Godolphin.' Mrs Aspley's face cleared instantly. 'So good of you to come and so promptly too. Perhaps you might be able to explain what strange scrape my stepdaughter has got herself into this time.'

Perhaps it was as well Diana had

been rendered speechless with indignation. Edgar Godolphin's eyes swept across the room, taking in all its occupants, and he raised a quizzical eyebrow.

'I shall do my best,' he said, bowing towards his hostess, but then turning a beady eye upon Mrs Brown. 'I did not expect to meet you again quite so soon, madam.'

'You know this woman?' Mrs Aspley asked, cutting short Mrs Brown's flustered murmur.

Mr Godolphin smiled wryly.

'We have met,' he said. 'It's not quite the same thing.'

And then all the explanations came out, while Diana squirmed almost as much as Mrs Brown.

'Oh dear, I really don't know what to do about all this,' Mrs Aspley fretted, once Mr Godolphin had finished. She gave her stepdaughter a covert glare for putting her in such a quandary.

'As I see it, there is only one thing we can do,' Mr Godolphin replied. 'We must call on Mrs Brown's patient and see how matters stand with her.'

* * *

Long before the journey's end, Mrs Aspley began to look as if she wished she had not been persuaded that this was a good idea. But Diana knew her stepmother had a stubborn streak that prevented her from countermanding her own orders once she had made up her mind on something.

The hackney coach plunged deeper and deeper into an insalubrious slum. Diana was appalled by the narrowness, darkness and dirt of the streets, the gaping roofs and broken windows, the ragged, barefoot children with runny noses and bowed legs, the elderly beggars and maimed soldiers with missing limbs.

'Really, you shouldn't venture any further,' Mrs Brown repeated over and over again. 'It's no place for the likes of you and everything will be at sixes and sevens . . . '

But Mr Godolphin assured her that they would excuse any mess. Diana's heart beat faster at the thought that her quest might finally be over. She clung tightly to Mrs Brown's arm once they had descended from the coach, terrified of losing their guide in this labyrinth.

Reluctantly Mrs Brown led the way into one of the tumbledown tenements and up a creaking staircase to the garrets. At the last door, she turned back towards the small party.

'Perhaps I'd best go in first,' she suggested. 'I could see that all was well and see how Miss Alice is faring and everything.'

With a flash of insight, Diana realised that poor Mrs Brown might be ashamed of the way she was forced to live, and perhaps worried too in case her husband was home.

'Of course. Go ahead.'

Diana did not relish being left on the landing with her stepmother and Edgar Godolphin. The former was clearly not best pleased with her and the latter had been throwing Diana odd, questioning looks that she did not know how to interpret.

'I hope for your sake, Diana, that this escapade will not end badly,' Mrs Aspley began, echoing Diana's secret fears.

Inside the garret, she could hear hasty movements, as if Mrs Brown was attempting to hide something she did not want them to see, and Diana heard her speaking in a low, soothing undertone as might be used to address an invalid.

A moment later, the door opened a crack, just far enough to allow Mrs Brown to poke her head round its edge.

'Really, sir, ladies, she's very bad at the moment. I don't think it'd be right to disturb her . . . ' she began.

Diana had risen on tiptoe to try to see past Mrs Brown. She caught a glimpse of a cupboard-bed with thread-bare curtains half-dragged from their rings.

'But she is awake, isn't she?' Mr Godolphin said. 'We heard you speaking to her.'

'Y-yes,' Mrs Brown admitted reluctantly, 'but . . . '

'Might I not say just a few words to her?' Diana pleaded. 'I'm sure she'll recognise my voice.'

Mrs Aspley murmured something about leaving, but Diana barely heard her, because at that moment, she heard something stir within the room.

Impatience got the better of her.

'Alice?' she called softly as she pushed open the door, catching Mrs Brown off guard.

Even Diana was taken aback to find herself already in the centre of the cramped room. But she saw nothing of the squalor around her, intent only on the curtained bed.

'It's me, Diana. I've come to help you . . . ' she went on, unnerved by the stillness of the room.

'Diana, come away at once.'

Mrs Aspley had stepped gingerly into

the garret. Diana glanced at her, torn. To come this close and not even get the slightest glimpse of Alice or just one word from her, after all Edgar Godolphin had said about the Browns being fraudsters . . .

'Tomorrow perhaps she'll be better,' Mrs Brown quavered.

Diana tried to swallow her disappointment. And then she heard a weak, mewling cry from the bed, a cry of pain or protest of someone too weak to speak. It was enough to make up her mind.

She darted the last few steps across the room and yanked aside the curtain.

Behind her, she heard her stepmother cry out, apparently shocked at her action, but Diana paid no attention. Instead her eyes were riveted to the occupants of the bed — a disgruntled-looking tabby cat with half-a-dozen blind kittens in a variety of mongrel colours.

As Diana stared in incomprehension, she heard footsteps tumbling down the creaking stairs. She whipped round. Only her stepmother was left in the room, leaning against the wall, as if she had been pushed aside by Mrs Brown in her precipitate flight.

No More Adventures

'Diana, come here at once! Mr Godolphin, where are you going? You cannot leave us here like this. Oh!'

Mrs Aspley seemed not to know in which direction to turn, desperate to pursue Mr Godolphin, but loath to leave her stepdaughter behind in such an unsavoury place.

Diana gathered her wits with an effort. She crossed the garret towards her stepmother, but she felt as unsteady as if she had been woken too suddenly from a dream.

'Where's Mr — ' she began, but Mrs Aspley's hysterical laugh cut her short.

'He ran after that woman. She knew she was going to be caught out and — ' Her breath caught in her throat in something that sounded uncannily like a hiccup.

Diana swallowed, but this was no

time to be paralysed by fear at the strange situation in which they found themselves.

'Let's go downstairs,' she said. 'I'm sure he won't go far and the hackney coach must still be outside.'

Clinging to each other for reassurance, they made their way back down the rickety stairs. Just as they reached the dingy hallway on the ground floor, the outer door opened to reveal Edgar Godolphin.

He shook his head at their questions and exclamations of relief.

'It's no good. She got away,' he said. 'She knows all the twists and turns of these alleys and I didn't dare follow too far, for fear of not being able to find my way back to you.'

His eyes fell unconsciously on Diana's face at the last word. She flushed, even though she knew he had meant nothing by that look.

She had half-expected him to reproach her for bringing them on this wild goose chase or gloat that his mistrust of the Browns had been justified. Instead he devoted himself to soothing Mrs Aspley's agitation and helping them both into the coach.

At first, Diana hardly heard a word that passed between the others on their return journey. Mrs Aspley was only too pleased to get away from that squalid part of town while they still had not been robbed or murdered or both and she was only sorry that Mrs Brown had escaped justice for the attempted fraud.

None of that was of any importance to Diana, not now she knew Edgar Godolphin was right and Mrs Brown, like her husband, had only been trying to cheat money out of her.

'I'm sorry. I've wasted everyone's time to no good end,' she burst out suddenly, because she would far rather the words were out in the open than festering inside her. 'If I had listened to you, sir . . . '

'It doesn't matter,' Edgar interrupted

soothingly. 'It was my suggestion that we should accompany Mrs Brown and put her story to the test.'

'I don't know what you were thinking of, sir, urging us to mix with such people,' Mrs Aspley chided, a sure sign she had been badly frightened because otherwise nothing would have induced her to turn upon someone as influential as Mr Godolphin.

'I'm sorry for that too, but there was a chance, however slim, that Mrs Brown was telling the truth. For Miss Aspley's sake, I was not prepared to leave any stone unturned in her quest for her friend.'

Diana felt another wave of warmth creep over her. It almost, almost sounded as if he cared for her more than common courtesy required.

Mrs Aspley pursed her lips, as if tempted to make some acidic remark about the nature of their quest. Instead she turned on her stepdaughter.

'Well, I hope at least, Diana, that you didn't give that woman any money.'

'N-not much,' Diana stammered, wishing she dared to lie and say she hadn't given anything. But hers was essentially an honest nature.

Mrs Aspley sighed.

'Oh, Diana, what am I going to do with you?'

Diana averted her face to hide the tears that clouded her eyes. It was not the money she begrudged. She would manage somehow with what little was left of her allowance. But now that her last hope of finding Alice was gone, suddenly her stepmother's chiding felt too much for her.

'I'm not saying it is not commendable to have a generous heart,' Mrs Aspley went on, 'but unless you exercise a little prudence, there will always be somebody who will exploit your good nature.'

Her tone was kinder than Diana was used to and it made it even harder for her to keep control of her emotions. Indeed a loud sob escaped her and she dug the heels of her hands in her eye sockets to push back the insistent tears.

'Here, take this,' a deep voice murmured.

Diana raised swimming eyes towards Mr Godolphin. He had leaned forward, so close that his knee brushed hers, to offer her a freshly laundered handkerchief.

'Th-thank you,' she said, trying to smile, but she was compelled to bite her lower lip to prevent herself from sobbing once more.

He smiled and it made him so heart-stoppingly handsome, Diana was forced to hide her face in the handkerchief, abashed by the sudden flood of emotion.

'At last,' Mrs Aspley exclaimed in relief as the carriage stopped outside their front door.

Edgar Godolphin descended first to help them alight. He squeezed Diana's fingers, as if to coax her to look up, but all she really wanted was to scuttle into the house and conceal her tear-blotched face.

And then a voice grated on her ear.

'Miss? Miss?'

Diana closed her eyes and instinctively clutched Mr Godolphin's hand tighter. She recognised Mrs Jones's voice. Coming on top of everything else, she could not cope with this too. Perhaps if she pretended she had not heard and hurried towards the house . . .

But Mrs Jones was not to be shaken off so easily.

'Miss, I've something to tell you,' she insisted, raising her voice as she scurried towards them.

In a single smooth movement, Mr Godolphin stepped around Diana, to form a physical barrier between her and the beggar-woman.

'Here, take my arm,' he said.

'Thank you,' Diana murmured, grateful, for once, that her stepmother was flanking her other side. The door had already been opened by an attentive servant. Only a few more yards and she would be safe.

But still Mrs Jones was not daunted. She was following them up the front path.

'I've news for you, Miss,' she insisted. 'About the errand you gave me.'

A wave of nausea overwhelmed Diana. She wanted to deny it all. She could not bear to have her hopes raised once more, only for them to be dashed. Her folly had already been exposed once this morning to Mrs Aspley and Mr Godolphin. What would they think of her now?

'You promised to pay me,' Mrs Jones's voice had risen to a screech. 'I've done what you said, when I could've been earning a crust some other way to feed the little 'uns.'

Her words made Diana hesitate. She glanced back for the first time, indecision gripping her. But Mrs Aspley took charge this time.

'Go away, or I'll call the watch and have you removed,' she said. It was obvious to Diana that she was mortified that, by encouraging the crone, her stepdaughter had made a spectacle of them in front of the whole square.

She tugged her stepdaughter into the house. At the same time, Diana heard Mrs Jones call out three more words, but in the bustle, she could not make out what they were.

It was too late in any case. The door thudded behind them. But Diana sensed that Mr Godolphin had suddenly stiffened. Nonetheless, at Mrs Aspley's invitation, he agreed to step into the drawing room.

Diana would have liked to slip away, but he prevented her by saying, 'Miss Aspley, there's something I wish to ask you before I go.'

His restrained tones, so unlike his warmth in the hackney coach, sent a chill to Diana's heart.

'Miss Aspley,' Mr Godolphin began in his most measured tone, 'am I right in deducing that you asked that woman to help you find Miss Simmonds?'

Diana reddened, conscious that her

stepmother too was waiting for her answer, ready to pounce. But there was no evading such a direct question.

'Yes,' she whispered.

'Oh, Diana, how could you?' Mrs Aspley broke in. 'To expose yourself, and me too, to all manner of plots and manipulations . . . '

A dreadful notion chilled Diana.

'You think Mrs Jones was part of the plot this morning?' she asked, her eyes darting from her stepmother to Mr Godolphin. 'You believe I brought all of this upon myself, don't you?'

Mrs Aspley's silence spoke volumes. But it was not her good opinion that Diana wanted most. Her eyes fixed upon Mr Godolphin's face, desperate for his approval.

'Well,' he drawled, 'if you did, then you were also the means of exposing the plot before you were bled dry, by making certain Mrs Brown did not escape before we had called her bluff.'

But Diana could take no comfort in his words. Not when he spoke with such restraint. She dropped her head silently.

Mr Godolphin stirred.

'I ought to be going,' he said. 'There are matters I must attend to.'

This was Mrs Aspley's cue to gush with gratitude and apologies for having taken up so much of his valuable time. Mr Godolphin cut her short as far as he could without appearing rude, before he extracted himself from the room.

'Well,' Mrs Aspley said, as soon as she was certain he was out of earshot, 'I hope, Diana, that this morning's adventures have put an end to your misguided quest.'

Diana sank dejectedly into a chair and didn't even notice that her stepmother did not chide her about her posture.

'Don't worry,' she said. 'I've learnt my lesson. There will be no more adventures, I promise.'

★ ★ ★

It was an uncharacteristically subdued Diana who was shown into the Godolphins' drawing room a few days later.

Unusually, Mrs Godolphin was alone when they arrived. Diana felt her spirits deflate a little further, though she hardly liked to admit, even to herself, that she had hoped Edgar Godolphin might be present. But of course he must have his own pursuits and could not be expected to dance attendance on his mother at all hours of the day.

After initial greetings had been exchanged, Diana found her attention drifting. The older women's voices sank into a lulling babble, until she was jolted awake by the sound of Mrs Duberry's name. She could hardly believe that her stepmother still had not realised that that episode too was connected with Alice.

'Ah, that's all very well,' Mrs Godolphin said, shaking her head. 'But sometimes all you need is somebody to do a little mending and minor alterations. If you ever need someone of that kind, let me recommend my own latest find.' She extended her arm towards Mrs Aspley. 'Would you believe I caught the sleeve of this gown on something and she managed to mend it so that you can hardly see the rip?'

Both Diana and her stepmother dutifully leaned closer to examine the minute, almost invisible stitching.

'It's rare to find workmanship of this quality,' Mrs Aspley agreed. 'I suppose she comes highly recommended?'

'Ah, you see, that's the irony. Heaven knows where my son found her. All I wanted was someone to hem a few sheets and it was quite by chance I discovered the poor girl was from a good family, but was forced to earn her bread after being cruelly deceived by a plausible villain, who inveigled her into a sham marriage and then deserted her when she found herself carrying his child.'

Something akin to hope stirred

within Diana. Then she pushed it down. No doubt London and every town was full of girls with a similar tale.

'Indeed. Perhaps you'll furnish me with her address,' Mrs Aspley replied, not wanting to look uncharitable or narrow-minded in comparison with Mrs Godolphin.

'I can do better than that,' their hostess replied. 'The girl is in the house at this very moment. I let her work here because I suspect she lives in some draughty garret and mercifully her little boy is not at all like my son was at that age and sleeps for much of the time, so neither of them disturbs the smooth running of the household.'

While she was speaking, Mrs Godolphin rang the bell.

Once more Diana felt a stirring of anticipation deep within her, which she suppressed with difficulty, afraid of being disappointed once more.

Her approach was heralded by the thin wail of a baby and a low, female voice desperately trying to shush the unhappy child. It was a refined voice, but Mrs Aspley pursed her lips in disapproval. The tap at the door was barely audible.

'Come in.'

'I'm sorry, madam, he wouldn't settle and I didn't like to keep you waiting . . . '

The seamstress began speaking before the door was fully open and she was still hidden from view. Diana's heartbeat quickened as a slight figure slid into the room and then stopped in confusion to find guests present.

Diana found herself unable to turn her gaze away or to move. Large blue eyes gazed back at her out of an unnaturally pale face. A single fair lock had escaped from the tight knot at the back of her head.

Diana felt a smile irradiate her face.

'Alice!' she exclaimed. 'At last! I've been looking for you everywhere.'

Diana darted across the room, but to

her dismay, Alice shrank back against the wall.

Diana had intended to embrace her, but she stumbled to a halt, unnerved by the numb way in which Alice was staring at her.

Somewhere behind her, Diana heard her stepmother draw in a sharp breath. Alice's eyes flickered across the room. She tightened her grip on the baby and dropped a subservient curtsey that cut Diana to the heart. The baby's cries had dwindled into exhausted hiccups and he bowed his red face upon his mother's shoulder.

'I'm sorry, madam, I didn't realise you were not alone,' Alice stammered, casting another frightened glance first at Diana, then at Mrs Aspley.

'Oh, never mind about that.' Mrs Godolphin dismissed her fears with a wave of the hand. 'These ladies are precisely why I summoned you.'

'Oh, I know you cannot have forgotten me,' Diana said, reaching out to clasp her friend's arm, though Alice still shrank from her.

'Please, Diana — Miss Aspley, you mustn't . . . ' she murmured, dropping her head.

'We swore we'd be friends always, no matter what happened,' Diana cut her short, hurt by the other girl's reticence. 'Why are you acting so strangely towards me?'

As she uttered the words, she saw the anguish in Alice's eyes and she realised what it meant. Alice's feelings had not changed. It was only the circumstances to which she had been reduced that had put barriers between them, making her feel she was no longer worthy of Diana's friendship. That, for Diana's sake, she ought to keep her distance, because she did not want her ruined reputation to taint her friend by association.

'Diana, I am not at all sure this is wise,' Mrs Aspley intervened, unease audible in her voice.

Alice turned towards her, grasping at

her words like a drowning man to a straw.

'Please don't worry, Mrs Aspley,' she said. 'I understand your reservations and I want you to know that I am not so selfish that I would jeopardise Di — Miss Aspley's marriage prospects by renewing our friendship.' She turned towards Diana as she continued in heartbroken tones, 'I know that when I leave this room, we must never meet again.'

'No!' Diana cried out. 'I won't let it happen.' She could not quite believe that she had spent so much time trying to find Alice, only for her friend to renounce her like this.

'That is not entirely true, Miss Simmonds,' a low, deep voice said.

Both young women started. Neither of them had heard the door brush open to admit Edgar Godolphin.

'I'm sorry for intruding like this,' he went on, 'but there is an unoccupied cottage on my estate in Derbyshire. It is at your disposal if you want it. You could live there quite privately, though you would, I fear, have to pass yourself off as a widow.'

Alice was staring at him with wide, almost frightened eyes.

'Oh, but I could not possibly accept such a generous offer from a stranger,' she stammered. 'How would I ever repay you?'

'By consenting to teach my tenants' children to read and write, and perhaps a little plain sewing for the girls.'

Diana thought Edgar Godolphin had never looked so handsome before, his face softened in entreaty, his eyes so tender that she scarce recognised him as the same man who had often barked at her in irritation.

Alice glanced at Diana, then back up at Mr Godolphin, and Diana could see a smile threatening to spread across her face.

'Thank you, sir,' Alice said, freeing one of her hands so she could clasp Mr Godolphin's fervently. 'You don't know what this means to me.'

'Oh, I know you won't regret this.' Diana could contain herself no longer. Grasping Mr Godolphin's sleeve for support, she stretched up on tiptoe and pecked him on the cheek.

'Diana!' Mrs Aspley gasped, as if she was about to faint.

★ ★ ★

Naturally Mrs Aspley had plenty to say to her stepdaughter about her behaviour during the carriage ride home, but for once Diana scarcely heard her.

It was not until after Alice had withdrawn from the room with little Ben that Diana had gathered enough wits to ask Mr Godolphin how he had found her friend.

'I didn't. *You* did. I mean I cannot take credit for something I didn't do,' Mr Godolphin replied. 'It was your idea to employ Mrs Jones.'

'Mrs Jones?' Diana felt as if she had been cuffed around the head.

'I take it that you didn't hear the last

words she called after you the other day?'

Diana shook her head.

'She said, 'I've found her.' That's why I hurried away from your house. I hoped Mrs Jones might still be loitering nearby. Fortunately she was and I managed to extract the whole story from her.'

'Oh.' Diana could scarcely take any of it in. 'But if you suspected then that she might know something, why didn't you tell me?'

'I didn't want to raise false hopes. I've seen you disappointed too many times during the last days.'

Again there was something about the way he uttered the words.

In parting, he had leaned closer to her and murmured in a low tone so her stepmother wouldn't hear, 'What, no kiss? I own I am disappointed, Miss Aspley.'

Naturally she reddened, though she gathered enough spirit to tap him on the arm with her fan and murmur back,

'It's wicked of you to tease me like that.'

His eyes lingered on her face and for once she was grateful when her stepmother whisked her away to dress for yet another ball.

In less than an hour, she would see Edgar again.

She whisked round to face her maid.

'I've changed my mind,' she said. 'I want to wear the new gown tonight.'

★   ★   ★

Diana sensed heads turning and eyes following her as she entered the ballroom. For once in her life, she knew she was beautiful.

Secretly, Diana hoped the new dress would give her the courage she needed, as well as perhaps showing Mr Edgar Godolphin that she wasn't just a child or just a friend.

Her eyes searched the crowd, as she gathered compliments and invitations to dance, but all the while she was looking for just one person. It gave her a jolt to catch sight of Mr Drake at the far end of the ballroom. But the man she strongly suspected of being Alice's seducer had apparently not seen her yet.

A minute more and she had forgotten that such a person existed. Because there was Edgar Godolphin, turned in profile, talking to an acquaintance. And then, incredibly, as if he had felt her gaze upon him, he turned his face towards her.

She saw him catch his breath. His expression changed. His eyes widened. And then her stepmother asked her a question and Diana was obliged to turn away from the man she realised somehow, implausibly, despite his faults, she had come to love.

Diana had no idea whether she answered her stepmother's question coherently. All such considerations were meaningless when she heard *that* voice close beside her.

'Twice in one day, Miss Aspley?'

Diana could not help glowing.

'So it would seem,' she replied.

'I suppose you are already engaged for every dance?' Mr Godolphin probed.

'Not quite.'

Grey-green eyes twinkled down at her. How could she have ever thought they were cold?

'Ah, then perhaps I ought to remedy that calamitous state of affairs. Would you deign to set aside a pair of dances for me too?'

'I might consider it,' she replied, but was struck by how much more difficult it was to behave naturally around him. Had she always blushed so much and felt this excited, frightened tightness in her chest when he was near?

Diana could not have told anyone afterwards how many dances she danced or with whom, or how many couples there were in the longways set. She could not seem to tear her gaze away from Edgar Godolphin. Even when they were separated by the dance, her eyes were drawn to him. When she was obliged to turn away from him, she sensed him behind her, as if they were connected by an invisible thread.

He cleared his throat.

'Miss Aspley,' he said with uncharacteristic diffidence, 'I wondered if I might be permitted to say something.'

For a moment, Diana felt a complete blank in her mind. And then her heart lurched with a hope she was forced to suppress, because if she were wrong, if she had misunderstood, she would *die* of disappointment.

'Certainly, sir.'

A wave of dizziness struck Diana, as if the whole world had diminished into a hum and a blur and the only real thing left was a pair of grey-green eyes.

And then she found herself spiralling back to earth again.

'Ah, Miss Aspley, you look more divine than ever.' Mr Beaumont smiled as he approached. 'If my heart had not already been hopelessly ensnared, I would be lost now.'

He emitted a sigh that broke Diana's heart.

'Oh, you must never despair,' she replied. 'Constancy is a virtue and, if all the conduct books and morality tales are to be believed, virtue is always rewarded.'

Mr Beaumont gave her a quizzical look, but his reply was interrupted by a cough.

'I'm not sure that things work out in real life exactly as they do in novels,' Mr Godolphin remarked. 'Nor is it so obvious who is a hero and who a villain.'

As so often before, Diana felt a prickle of antagonism pass between the two gentlemen. Nonetheless, Mr Beaumont laughed.

'Very true. But come, this is far too grave a subject for the ballroom. Are you free to dance the next dances with me, or am I doomed to have my heart broken once more?'

There was something about the way Mr Beaumont uttered the last phrase that gave Diana a strange jolt. Perhaps it was no more than her imagination playing tricks. She had felt unlike herself all evening. Either way, she loved dancing far too much to refuse.

And yet, she couldn't resist casting a look back at Edgar Godolphin as Mr Beaumont led her towards the centre of the room. Their eyes met briefly, but Mr Godolphin was the first to turn away, leaving Diana oddly bereft.

She rallied as best she could. She would have liked to tell Mr Beaumont that they had found Alice, but her partner barely left her an opening in the conversation. And yet, it seemed to Diana that his cheerfulness was forced and that underneath it, something was troubling him.

His expression darkened whenever they encountered Mr Drake in the course of their dances. It strengthened Diana's resolve to speak out, but when they reached the foot of the set during their second dance, Mr Beaumont forestalled her.

'Miss Aspley,' he said in an urgent whisper, 'would you have any objection if we did not dance up the set again? I know it is contrary to etiquette, but there is something of the utmost urgency that I must say to you.

'Perhaps you could pretend to be unwell?' Mr Beaumont suggested when she hesitated too long.

'Yes. Of course.' Surely not even Mrs Aspley could object to that, Diana added silently.

He led her to a secluded seat in a window embrasure and extracted her fan from her fingers so he might cool her face.

'At last,' he breathed. Mr Beaumont seized her hand and raised it to his lips.

'Oh!' she exclaimed in surprise. She had not expected such demonstrativeness, at least not until she had given him her news. Or was it possible that he already knew and wished to thank her for helping to rescue Alice?

'Forgive my impetuosity, Miss Aspley,'

he continued in the same fervent tone. 'My feelings are too strong for my discretion. But you must be aware of how much I adore you.'

Diana blinked at him like a half-fledged owlet. But he was kissing her hand again and she had not the slightest idea what to do.

'I'm afraid I don't understand,' she faltered.

'Your innocence and modesty are bewitching,' he went on. 'I have not been able to stop thinking about you since our first meeting.'

Rather more roughly than she had intended, Diana snatched her hand out of his grasp.

'Now I know you must be teasing me,' she said, but Mr Beaumont did not respond to her smile or her nervous laugh. 'Oh, but what about Alice?' she blurted out.

'Alice?'

In any other circumstances, his blank look would have been comical. Even now Diana struggled to suppress hysterical giggles.

'Alice Simmonds, my best friend,' she prompted him. 'Your one true love?'

And suddenly the situation wasn't comical any more. Diana saw her companion's expression darken. His eyes took on a guarded, suspicious look.

'Miss Simmonds is dead,' he said with stiff lips. 'Surely you don't expect me to spend the rest of my life . . . '

'Oh, but she isn't,' Diana couldn't help bursting in. 'She's alive and we found her and . . . '

Her voice caught in her throat. She had expected Mr Beaumont to be incredulous, relieved, overjoyed. His face showed none of those emotions. She couldn't quite decipher the expression in his eyes, but all of a sudden, she felt frightened, as if under threat. She barely noticed that the music had stopped and the volume of conversation had increased as the longways set broke up.

Mr Beaumont averted his face and pressed his hand to his forehead.

'No,' he whispered. 'That this should happen now, when I thought — hoped I might have found happiness again.'

Diana's heart squeezed tight in panic. Surely she could not have inadvertently stolen the heart of the man she had hoped would marry her best friend? There had to be some way back.

'If you could only see Alice, she has hardly been changed at all by her ordeal,' Diana ventured. 'She is still the kind, gentle creature she always was . . .'

He turned upon her with a fierce look that made her breath catch.

'Can you not see it is too late?' he declared. 'Whatever it was that I felt for Miss Simmonds, it pales into insignificance beside what I feel for you?'

Diana recoiled in horror. This was worse than she had ever dreamed in her darkest nightmares.

'Sir, you must not say such things. You barely know me.'

'I cannot help the way I feel,' he

interrupted her, 'and after all the encouragement you have given me, I fancy you are not entirely indifferent towards me.'

'Encouragement?' Diana stammered. 'I assure you, I never intended — it never even crossed my mind that you might misinterpret . . . oh, heavens, what am I going to do?'

She could see the truth dawning on Mr Beaumont, his eyes taking on that same hard, guarded look.

'Am I to understand that you have been merely toying with me?'

'No, I — '

But Diana's protest was cut short.

'Good evening, Miss Aspley.'

The voice did not strike Diana as familiar and she sprang back when she looked up and encountered the sardonic gaze of Mr Drake. She had forgotten how tall and imposing he was.

'Ah, Beaumont, I haven't seen you in an age,' he went on imperturbably. 'How is your wife?'

Vicious Rumours

The colour drained from Mr Beaumont's face. 'My — my wife?' he echoed.

'Yes, your wife,' Mr Drake repeated. 'You *do* have one, don't you, tucked away in the countryside, out of harm's way? It took me quite a while to discover her existence. Quite the recluse, isn't she?'

There was an edge to Mr Drake's tone that suggested that Mrs Beaumont's exile might not have been voluntary.

'I — I — this is preposterous,' Mr Beaumont was visibly struggling to find the right words. 'I pray you, do not believe a word this man says, Miss Aspley. There is not a whit of truth in any of it.'

Diana couldn't reply. Whom should she believe? She didn't know either man well enough to tell which of them was lying.

Hadn't Mrs Godolphin said something about Alice being inveigled into a false marriage? Diana had assumed that meant the man who conducted the ceremony had not been ordained or that there was some other irregularity. But what if Alice had been tricked into marriage by a bigamist and that man proved to be Mr Beaumont . . .

Mr Godolphin never trusted him, a voice whispered in her ear.

'I would not make such claims if I couldn't prove them,' Mr Drake was saying. 'I have a copy of the marriage licence . . . '

'Obviously a forgery,' Mr Beaumont butted in. 'I told you this man would stop at nothing . . . '

'And, of course, the lady herself is in my care at present,' Mr Drake continued as if the other man had not spoken. 'I've offered her my services as a lawyer to obtain a legal separation and a modicum of the independence of which she has been deprived for far too long.'

'Miss Aspley, you are looking quite faint. Can I be of any assistance?'

Edgar Godolphin's voice revived Diana. Her head shot up and instinctively she clutched his arm with both hands.

'Oh, sir, please take me away from here.'

Mr Beaumont was not willing to let her go without making one final appeal.

'Ah, Miss Aspley, will you not give me one chance to explain before you break my heart?'

She turned away before he could catch her eye. She didn't want to see him again. Was he even aware his last words were a tacit admission of guilt?

'Can you bear to tell me what has distressed you so?' Edgar Godolphin asked softly.

'Did you know that Mr Beaumont is married?' Diana asked in a thin, strained voice unlike her own.

As she uttered the words, she felt Mr Godolphin start and she sensed his gaze upon her face, though she was staring straight ahead.

'I'd heard rumours that he had been married once, but nobody knew whether his wife was alive or dead,' he replied. 'There were rumours of ill-treatment, for the most part discredited, but persistent enough to strike me as worrying.'

'And yet you did not see fit to warn me?' A rare flash of temper ignited in her.

'Would you have believed me?' he countered.

Diana dropped her head.

'No, I don't suppose I would,' she admitted.

'If it is any consolation, you are by no means the only person to be taken in by Beaumont's charm,' Mr Godolphin said. 'I've known people twice your age, who consider themselves to be men and women of the world who have been deceived by him.' Then, changing his tone to a much brisker, brighter one, he added, 'And now, Miss Aspley, at the risk of getting ourselves gossiped about, would you care to dance the last dances before suppertime with me?'

Diana mustered a smile.

'I should be delighted,' she said.

In the days that followed, however, Diana saw nothing of Edgar Godolphin. Moreover, his mother was exceedingly vague about the nature of the business that was apparently keeping him so busy.

Diana's ear was so attuned to any mention of his name that it was not surprising that one evening in the drawing room of one of her stepmother's friends, her attention was caught by two ladies gossiping nearby, while they waited for the gentlemen to join them.

'What has become of Mr Edgar Godolphin? I haven't seen him in an age.'

'Haven't you heard? They say he has a mistress with whom he is completely besotted.'

A dart of pain sliced through Diana.

For a moment, she could not even breathe.

'No? Really? And he always struck me as so aloof and proper.'

'Ah, well, you know what they say, it's always the quiet ones you have to watch. By all accounts his fallen angel is a very pretty seamstress, genteelly born too, if what they say is true.'

Diana let out a surreptitious sigh of relief. Of course it was inevitable that petty-minded people would misunderstand Mr Godolphin's motives in rescuing Alice. Diana even felt guilty at having tarnished his good name like this.

Amid all these thoughts, Diana missed the other woman's reply.

'What's more, it seems like it might be a longstanding arrangement,' the informant resumed. 'The girl has, I believe, a child of five or six months of age.'

Unlike these malicious tabbies, she knew exactly how sweet-natured and beautiful Alice was. Why shouldn't Mr

Godolphin fall in love with her? And if he was high-minded enough to rescue Alice from the gutter, why should he not marry her too?

'But what about Miss Aspley? I heard he was courting her — or at any rate he has been seen in her company a good deal.'

Diana shrank deeper into the shadows. The women could not have been aware that she was seated so close to them.

'Oh, *that* cannot be anything very serious, not with a giddy little thing like her. I'm sure she's flighty enough not to take it too much to heart if he does throw her over.'

Was that really how people regarded her? Diana bit her lip and blinked, determined that nobody would see her cry.

Of course Alice is better suited to Edgar Godolphin, fallen woman or not, Diana told herself. I am far too impetuous. He probably still regards me as an amusing child. And if he does marry Alice, I shall have to pretend to be glad when they tell me of their engagement. And I shall be. I shall because they deserve to be happy.

I shall bleed to death inside, but I'll smile while I do it and nobody will ever, ever know. But oh, it will be hard.

She managed not to cry until she reached the privacy of her bedroom that night. Instead she put on her brightest smile and launched herself into as much repartee as she could so nobody would guess that anything ailed her.

'You seemed in high spirits tonight,' her stepmother remarked in the carriage on the way back.

'Did I?' Diana asked, riding the waves of a fresh flood of pain. She had no idea how she managed to keep her voice so steady.

But she cried herself to sleep that night. At breakfast the following morning, she felt as sluggish as if someone had beaten her around the head. She barely paid any attention when a servant brought in a hand-delivered note for her stepmother.

'Well, Diana,' Mrs Aspley said, after a cursory skim, 'you will have to entertain yourself this morning. Mr Godolphin has asked to speak to me about a very delicate matter.'

A flare of hope lit up inside Diana and died just as quickly. It was evident that Mr Godolphin had no wish to see her and might not even stay long.

Nevertheless, she listened for his knock at the front door, the servant's footsteps in the hall, the sound of his voice, asking to speak to Mrs Aspley.

For once Diana was alone in the drawing room, her stepmother having elected to receive the visitor in the library. To take her mind off what might or might not be happening downstairs, Diana opened the pianoforte and settled down to practise. Her music master had always accused her of playing with more vigour and expression than accuracy, and today was no exception. Secretly she hoped the music might be audible in the room below and act as a reminder of her existence.

She didn't hear the footsteps on the stairs and was startled when the door opened behind her. Her first thought was that she had not heard Mr Godolphin depart and she was disappointed that she had not had a chance to dash to the window and catch a glimpse of him.

'I hope I am not intruding.'

At the sound of that masculine voice, Diana's hands jumped on the keyboard, producing a clashing discord. She turned as she rose from the piano stool.

'Gracious, Mr Godolphin, I was not expecting you,' she said and despised herself for sounding so girlishly fluttering.

'I'm sorry. I didn't mean to startle you.' He hovered near the door, as if uncertain whether to retreat or advance. 'I'll go away if you prefer.'

Diana's heart was beating frantically against her stays. Why was he here on his own? There was no sign of her stepmother. But she couldn't be rude to Mrs Aspley's guest.

'No, no, do come in. I've been wanting to ask you the latest news about Alice.' The last sentence came out in a rush because she knew that if she did not say it quickly, she might not be able to say it at all.

'Ah, yes.' Edgar Godolphin cleared his throat. 'There has been something of a change of plan about that.'

Diana's heart contracted.

So it was true. She thought she had prepared herself for this, but she realised now how much she had still allowed herself to hope.

Mr Godolphin closed the door and crossed the room towards her. But he stopped a few paces short of her, perhaps because she had flinched at the thought of being so close to him again.

'You will probably accuse me of keeping you in the dark again,' he said. 'But it was a delicate matter and the happiness of more than one person was at stake . . . '

I ought to be happy, not sick and miserable. Diana forced a smile to her lips, but she suspected it was a poor attempt.

'Oh, I am sure nothing you do can ever be wrong,' she said.

'Trust me, I am as fallible as the next man.'

Edgar Godolphin took a step closer and suddenly Diana was pulsingly aware of his proximity. His height, the breadth of his shoulders, his self-conscious smile, which reminded her of how he had looked just after she had kissed him . . .

No, she must not think about that.

Instead she turned aside, pretending to tidy an already neat stack of sheet music.

'If there is anyone you ought to thank, it is Mr Drake,' he went on.

'Mr Drake?' Diana echoed, glancing up.

'I sought him out after the ball. He was only too eager to tell me what manner of man Beaumont is and to warn me to protect you because another lady of his acquaintance had not been so fortunate. He blamed himself for not having warned her of his suspicions and quarrelling with her instead of making the declaration he had intended to make.'

A ripple ran down Diana spine. She didn't quite dare let herself hope. Not until he had spoken the words.

'Well, one thing led to another and the upshot is — ' Edgar Godolphin took a deep breath before he continued — 'with my mother's help, I have reintroduced Mr Drake to Miss Simmonds and he has managed to persuade her that her past is unimportant to him and that he is willing to bring up little Ben as if he was his own son.'

'Oh.' Diana scarcely noticed the sheaf of sheet music slip through her fingers and whisper to the floor. 'Oh, thank you. You have no idea how much this means to me.'

She grasped his sleeves and pulled

herself up on tiptoe and it was only at the last second that she realised that she had almost kissed him again and drew back, her cheeks blazing.

'Heavens, look at the mess!'

Diana dropped to her knees as she spoke, attempting to gather the sheets of music into some kind of order. She was relieved she had a good excuse not to look at Edgar Godolphin just yet.

Again she wondered where her stepmother was. It was not the custom for a young lady and an eligible bachelor to be left unchaperoned for long.

'I hoped you'd be pleased.' Edgar Godolphin's voice came from far, far above her. 'But there is another matter I wished to speak to you about. One of a delicate nature . . . '

His voice trailed away as Diana's heartbeat accelerated. That same word he had used in his note to Mrs Aspley. Could he mean . . . ?

Giddy little thing, a poisonous voice whispered in her ear. That's what

275

people think of you. That's what Mr Godolphin thinks of you. He probably wants to let you down gently.

In her haste, she spilled half the papers she had only just gathered up.

'Oh, bother! I'm all fingers and thumbs today, I scarcely know what I'm doing.' The words fell so quickly from Diana's lips that her sentences blended together.

'Can't you leave that for a moment?' He was beginning to sound irritable, though she was acutely aware that he was now crouched beside her.

'It won't take a second. And my stepmother would be so cross if — '

She gasped as a strong, masculine hand closed around her wrist.

'Blast it all, do you dislike me so much that you are incapable of staying still and listening while I am trying to propose to you?'

Diana froze. She cast a look up at his face, then down at the powerful fingers circling her wrist. Clearly Mr Godolphin misunderstood her glance, because he unclenched his fingers and rose. It was all Diana could do not to snatch his hand to detain him.

'Pro-propose?' she stammered. 'To — to *me*?'

Mr Godolphin dropped his chin and turned aside, as if to hide. Feeling too much at a disadvantage in terms of height, Diana scrambled to her feet, although several sheets of music were still scattered on the floor.

'Yes, yes, I know, it surprises me as much as it surprises you,' he said, almost sounding irritable as he strode away to the window. 'But the truth is I have grown — ' he cleared his throat — 'fond of you.'

'Fond?' Diana echoed, still feeling the blankness of shock, but aware of other emotions stirring within her. Doubt, hope, incredulity, but most of all fear. Fear that she had mishandled the situation and he would change his mind. And fear that she had misunderstood, or that it was merely fondness that he felt and nothing more.

'Well, fond is perhaps the wrong word,' Mr Godolphin admitted and Diana's heart plummeted. 'I have grown exceedingly attached to you. You might even say — ' his chin dropped even lower — 'that I . . . love you.'

Diana swallowed with difficulty, unable to take her eyes off his face, willing him to look at her. And when he did, she knew there was only one thing she could do. Casting the handful of sheet music onto the couch, she darted across the room and snatched both his hands.

'Do you really mean that?' she whispered, unable to raise her voice.

Her eyes roved across his face, which, because of her proximity, he could no longer hide from her. Her lips kept wanting to twitch into a smile and yet she did not quite dare. As Mr Godolphin's eyes locked at last on hers, she could see the same hesitancy in his expression. His fingers tightened round hers.

'Oh yes, I mean it,' he replied. 'More

than you know. More than I can say. No matter how exasperating your impetuosity can be, it is also endearing and — enchanting.'

'Oh.' Diana did not know whether to be exhilarated or insulted by his words. 'I don't believe any girl ever received such an unromantic declaration before.' She pretended to pout and made a half-hearted attempt to wrench her hands free, but this time Edgar Godolphin clung on.

'No, I don't suppose any have,' he admitted. 'But you are not like most girls. And I had hoped . . . ' He broke off again, as if he could not breathe.

'Go on,' she urged, squeezing his fingers.

'I had hoped you might have grown — fond of me too?' His intonation turned his words into a question.

The smile could not be repressed any longer. Nay more, Diana found she was giggling irresistibly.

'Are you *laughing* at me, madam?' His tone might have been angry, but looking into his eyes, Diana could see Edgar Godolphin was laughing too.

'N-no,' she stammered between giggles. 'It's — it's just that — '

She never got any further. All of a sudden, both her hands had been tucked behind her back so Edgar Godolphin could pull her to his chest without releasing her even for a second.

Her head whipped upward, her eyes wide with surprise, but she only formed the haziest impression of his face, because his lips were suddenly pressed against hers, stifling the last of her giggles.

'Mr Godolphin!' she gasped the second he raised his head, freeing her lips.

'What, you think you are the only one capable of being impulsive?' he asked. And then his expression grew graver. 'So, will you marry me? Do you love me?'

'Yes, yes, yes.'

He released her hands, but his arms wrapped further around her, while her fingers tentatively crept up his chest to twine about his neck. He gathered her in closer, closer, as he bent his head to kiss her again.

'And by the way,' he added, 'call me Edgar.'

THE END

We do hope that you have enjoyed reading this large print book.

Did you know that all of our titles are available for purchase?

We publish a wide range of high quality large print books including:
Romances, Mysteries, Classics
General Fiction
Non Fiction and Westerns

Special interest titles available in large print are:
The Little Oxford Dictionary
Music Book, Song Book
Hymn Book, Service Book

Also available from us courtesy of Oxford University Press:
Young Readers' Dictionary
(large print edition)
Young Readers' Thesaurus
(large print edition)

For further information or a free brochure, please contact us at:
Ulverscroft Large Print Books Ltd.,
The Green, Bradgate Road, Anstey,
Leicester, LE7 7FU, England.
Tel: (00 44) 0116 236 4325
Fax: (00 44) 0116 234 0205